The Great London Adventure

Neil Shaw-Larkman

The Great
London Adventure

International Media Developments Limited (1990 - 2001) & Neil Shaw-Larkman

An International Media Developments Limited Book

First Published in Great Britain by
International Media Developments Limited in 2001

This Paperback edition published in 2001 By

International Media Developments Publishing Limited
26 Priestgate
Peterborough
Cambridgeshire
PE1 1WG

ISBN: 0-9540371-0-3

Printed and bound in Great Britain by
Biddles Ltd
www.biddles.co.uk

Author's Note

Five years of development have passed and now the end is in sight. The publication of the Great London Adventure is about to be released.

I would like to offer my most sincere thanks to the staff at all of the London attractions that are featured in this book. Without your support research for this book would have been impossible. A special thank you to David Cope, Raven Master at the Tower Of London. You gave me a true insight into the world of ravens and their unique behaviour; they really are characters and I have had hours of pleasure watching them.

To embark on this venture was from the outset going to be a challenge. Little did I know how much of a challenge! Throughout the business community many have offered good advice and assistance and I thank you all. However, I would like especially to acknowledge Grant Thornton and Business Link Northampton.

The NSPCC in the United Kingdom is a very worthwhile charity. Through its work many children have been helped and their lives have changed for the better. As the author I have decided to donate some of the proceeds from the sale of this book to the NSPCC in the hope that children can be supported and helped through the charity whatever their needs are. All problems that children have should be heard. The correct authorities need to be accessible to assist in solving those problems and charities like the NSPCC need to be kept going. Their work really does make a difference. The NSPCC are totally dependent on donations to enable their child protection teams to continue their good work. Thank you for buying this book and helping us to enable the NSPCC to continue its fight to protect children.

I hope you enjoy the Great London Adventure and have as much fun reading the adventures of Fred, Charlie, Belvedere and all their friends as I have had writing about them.

A Special thank you to Tracey.

Neil Shaw - Larkman

To all the friends that have helped me succeed

And to the people who have helped donate to the children in need

I thank you all from the bottom of my heart

You all have played a very important part

1
chapter
Our journey begins

High in the sky above London the sun cast its heat like a covering blanket. But nothing could stop the fun two young ravens were having. Below people went about their business in the usual flurry of activity as the two ravens dived down just above their heads and swooped between lampposts before soaring back up high into the sky only to swoop down again.

The mischievous ravens that were causing all this trouble were called Fred and Charlie. They had began their lives high on the roof of the British Telecom Tower. Learning to fly had been a task that Fred and Charlie had only just mastered and not before collecting many bumps and bruises.

Now, with very little flying experience, they were out and about exploring the vast city of their birthplace, London. Great care had to be taken, however, as Fred and Charlie's landing's were not very good at all.

Upon this very morning, unbeknown to Fred and Charlie, their lives were about to be changed. Following a short rest on the roof of Buckingham Palace and a brief argument with a television arial on landing the two brothers decided to head off to their favourite place, the fountains of Trafalgar Square.

With a bank around this corner and a dive under a few lampposts Fred and Charlie were soon splashing about in the fountains and having a wonderful time. Many of the tourists stopped to look as Fred showed off, splashing his brother with his wing. The two brothers were having so much fun that neither of them noticed their father arrive with a great swoosh of his wings. Fred and Charlie's father enjoyed watching his sons have so much fun but he was not there to praise them on their splashing expertise.

Fred and Charlie's father clapped his wings together in order to gain his sons' attention. They waded over to see him.

"Hello, father, what are you doing here?" questioned Fred and Charlie who now were quite out of breath and concerned that they might be in trouble. Fred tried to remember if he had tidied the nest before they had left earlier that morning. Without delay their father told them to gather round and began to explain the reason for his visit.

"Now then, sons, the time has come for you to take some form of responsibility. You can not spend the rest of your lives playing in fountains and swooping about the streets. There is work to be done and you have to learn what being a raven is all about." Fred and Charlie looked at each other. Was this to be the end of the hours of fun and frolics? As a bead of sweat ran down their beaks their father continued, "Over the years I have told you about my work at the Tower of London as a raven guard. Well, now the time has come for you to learn the art of guarding such an important place and for you to follow in my footsteps as I did in my father's footsteps. There is much to be gained from guarding such a historical city as London, especially from the Tower of London. I want you to report to Hector, the chief of all the ravens at the Tower. He will explain your training and I shall see you after it is completed. I am sure you will make me proud of you and good luck." Without giving Fred and Charlie the chance to argue their father took to the air and flew across Trafalgar Square only glancing back at his sons once.

Fred and Charlie, who seemed to be in a state of shock, sat with their feet dangling in the cool waters of the fountain. Why did they have to go to work at the Tower? They would miss out on all the fun and the tales of the travelling birds that visited London every day. Charlie sat with his head hung low whilst Fred plucked at a ring pull from a discarded can that had become caught in his claw. Why was it no one considered the animals when they threw their rubbish away! The two brothers were so sad about the news their father had just broken to them they even refused crumbs being offered to them by passers by.

Taking a deep sigh Fred nudged his brother to attract his attention, but Charlie was deep in thought, so with a scoop of his wing Fred soaked his brother from head to foot. This soon brought Charlie to his senses.

"Ah, come on, Charlie, it might not be as bad as you think. Let's make a move as we don't want to be late on our first day and upset this Hector. We could end up polishing raven claws for the rest of the week."

Charlie, who was still drying himself off, agreed with Fred. He stretched his wings and in no time at all Fred and Charlie were in the air again.

The air swished through their feathers as below them the sights of London flickered by. Suddenly Fred noticed that they were over St James's Park and was convinced they were going in the wrong direction, but before he had time to mention this to his brother he noticed a brilliant light shining from a bush below. Charlie had also noticed the bright light and turned to his brother.

"Did you see that, Fred, what was it?"

"I saw it, Charlie, I saw it. Look, there it is again."

Charlie seemed very excited about the light and could hardly contain his curiosity. Fred suddenly noticed that his brother was no longer flying next to him, but heading down towards the bush. Fred took the position of a dive-bomber and set off after his brother.

Fred and Charlie circled the bush at great speed. The light seemed to be getting brighter. Although they both knew that they should be reporting to Hector at the Tower, this seemed more interesting and much more important. Fred tried to persuade his brother to leave the light alone, but Charlie was having none of it.

Their landing was not graceful at all, and having just missed a large tree Fred and Charlie ended up hanging upside down in a bush. Dusting themselves down and trying to hide the embarrassment of such a terrible landing Fred and Charlie made their way to the bush of the shining light.

Just as the two brothers approached the bush the shining light flashed once again. This time Fred and Charlie had to cover their eyes with their wings, as the light was so bright. Then as they lowered their wings they saw a tiny green man sat on the root of the large bush holding a piece of mirror. It was difficult to see who was more scared — Fred, Charlie or the Green Man who now stood with his hands on his hips.

"Oh great, just great, trust me to find two daft birds to come to my rescue. I shall never get home now. NEVER. That's it. The Great Gob will never speak to me again. Anyway, what am I doing talking to two birds with brains the size of peas, what am I thinking of?" With that the little green man sat back down and kicked a match that lay at his feet.

Fred was not sure, but he thought he saw a tiny tear run off the little green man's nose. Charlie however was unconcerned about the tear. How dare this little man talk to them this way? With a ruffle of his feathers and a puff of his chest Charlie stepped forward.

"Look you, whoever you might be, we came down to see what the light was all about and not to be spoken to like this, you piece of camel spit." Charlie felt very pleased with himself, he

5

had never spoken to anyone like this before and to make sure that his point had been made Charlie stuck his beak high into the air and gave his brother a reassuring nod. Fred just looked at his brother in disbelief and knew that Charlie had no idea what camel spit was. As always Charlie had overheard this saying and just repeated it.

The little green man once again got to his feet. "So you can understand me. I am so sorry about being rude and calling you names, but I am so worried. Please let me introduce myself. I am Belvedere and I am a Gronkiedoddle. I live under London in the many disused railway tunnels with thousand of other Gronkiedoddles."

Just as Belvedere was about to continue Charlie raised his wing and stopped him. "Hang on, underground tunnels, Gronkiedoddles. This is London. What are we talking about here? Sounds like a load of rubbish to me."

Then much to Charlie's and Fred's surprise Belvedere burst into laughter, so much so that he nearly tripped over his root. Charlie, however, found this most annoying and clawed at the dust with his foot. Finally Belvedere calmed himself down and shook his head from side to side.

"You two really are very young ravens. You obviously have not heard about the Gronkiedoddles and The Great Gob. Now he is a very important man. He is after all the ruler of all the animals in London, and that includes you." Fred suddenly realised that his father had mentioned The Great Gob in their bedtime stories and his beak fell open. Charlie noticed that his brother seemed shocked and before he could speak Fred placed his wing over his beak as Belvedere continued.

"We Gronkiedoddles do a very important job, you know. We help all the homeless children that live on the streets of London and all the children that have problems at home. We hope to bring inspiration and in some cases the difference between life and death. Once we have visited and done all we can to help we leave a cinnamon stick to prove that we were not part of their imagination. Care for one?" With that Belvedere pulled from his top pocket a cinnamon stick. Fred and Charlie decided not to take the gift as their father had always told them not to accept presents from strangers. Belvedere shrugged his shoulders and moved closer as he continued.

"Last night I had to go to Piccadilly Circus to help some of the homeless children there. But as it was getting light, I thought I had better make my way home. I must have taken a wrong turning, because before I knew where I was, I was stuck here in this bush and it was broad daylight. You see I can't let any human adults see me. I mean what would they think, a green man no taller than a few inches high running about. So when I saw you two ravens flying above I thought that you would be heading to the Tower of London where I know there is an entrance to one of our tunnels. Do you think you could give me a lift, please?" Another tear rolled off the end of Belvedere's nose. This time there was no doubt. Fred felt very sorry for the little chap and Charlie felt quite guilty and ashamed for his outburst earlier. So they both placed a wing tip around Belvedere's shoulder to comfort him.

Charlie explained that he and his brother were off to the Tower of London to train as raven guards and were glad to give him a lift. Fred, who had become a little emotional at seeing Belvedere upset, agreed by nodding his head whilst wiping a tear from his own eye with his other wing tip.

Fred and Charlie watched as a large grin spread across Belvedere's face. Suddenly the tiny little man got to his feet and began to do a funny little dance followed by a somersault.

"Brilliant, brilliant, one day I shall thank you by baking a huge cinnamon stick pie. Oh thank you so much. Yippee."

When Fred and Charlie saw that Belvedere was so happy they felt that they could not explain to him that they had never carried passengers before. Fred whispered into Charlie's ear that he had better take Belvedere with him as he was slightly larger and stronger so he could handle the extra weight. Charlie agreed with an air of importance.

With Belvedere griping tightly to Charlie's feathers and slightly hidden Fred and Charlie, made their way out from the cover of the bush and onto the grass of St James's Park. Many people had gathered by this time, sitting around in the deck-chairs enjoying the summer sun as this was a very popular spot for people to come and relax. With all these people Fred and Charlie were left with the problem of finding a suitable place to take off.

Suddenly Charlie noticed a clear passage through all the deck-chairs that looked like a runway at an airfield. It was perfect for their take off and he hoped that Fred would agree. Fred could see no other place and although he was not happy with all the people sitting so close to the runway, he agreed. Fred and Charlie made their way to the beginning of the long clear strip of grass between the deck-chairs. Charlie, as always, began to imagine that he was in the movies and Fred simply went along with his brother.

"Flight 101 ready for take off, check," shouted Charlie.

"Check and roger that, good buddy, ready for take off on runway three, systems are clear, weather is fine, but watch out for the cross winds. See you up there, Charlie."

"That's roger and out," replied Charlie, beginning to make the sound of an old war-plane.

Belvedere was not very comfortable at all and was trying to get used to the smelled of Charlie's feathers that smelt of old socks. He wondered what on earth Fred and Charlie were talking about. Little did he know that when they were young ravens they used to watch television through one of the big shop windows on Regent Street. It was a special treat for them if they had been good and because they could not hear the sound Charlie used to make up his own sounds and had become fascinated with the movies.

Then without warning Charlie started to run, nearly making Belvedere lose his grip. With wings flapping and tongues hanging out the two brothers headed off down their runway between the deck chairs. Belvedere was convinced they were not going to get into the air, but to his surprise Charlie slowly began to fly upward into the London sky only just missing a large tree.

"Phew, that was close, Charlie," shouted Fred.

"Head for the Thames and we will go down the river. That way we will not have to bank round too much to avoid buildings and Belvedere won't fall off."

Charlie agreed and shouted that he would follow as he was finding it very difficult to fly with the extra weight of Belvedere. Belvedere however clung on with his eyes shut tight. He was convinced they were not going to make it, but little did he know that Charlie was more worried about how they were going to land.

In no time at all the great landmark of the Tower of London lay ahead surrounded by buildings old and new.

"Keep your eyes open for a good spot to land, I don't want to hurt our passenger and I am getting tired now," shouted Charlie, quite out of breath and feeling very exhausted. Fred agreed and muttered under his breath that it would have been safer to land at Heathrow Airport.

Suddenly Fred let out a cry. "Look, Charlie, down there, that will do and it is in the grounds of the Tower. Come on, let's make a landing that will astonish Hector." Neither Belvedere nor Charlie liked the sound of making an astonishing landing but it was too late as Fred was already heading down to the landing spot.

"Hang on, Belvedere, this could be a rough landing," shouted Charlie as he followed his brother, but Belvedere was too frightened to look and clung on with all his might. Fred and Charlie glided down with their claws outstretched so that they could get as much of a grip as possible on what looked like very slippery grass.

Out of control and squawking at the top of their voices, the two brothers skidded across the grass with their wings flapping frantically in the hope that they could stop before they crashed into the bushes or, even worse, the wall. With beaks open wide Fred and Charlie realised where their dramatic landing was going to end — the flower-bed that looked so glorious with its red, white and blue flowers. Finally the two brothers and Belvedere came to an abrupt stop. Looking behind them they could see the deep tracks in the lawn where their claws had tried to grip.

Fred and Charlie were both upside down with their legs in the air. Fred was the first to speak, having removed all the flowers from his beak.

"Well, that did not go to well, did it, Charlie, AHHH

CHOOOO," sneezed Fred, removing the last tulip from the corner of his beak. Charlie, however, was not listening as he also was removing the many flowers that he had scooped up with his beak. Fred had to chuckle as his brother looked like a giant flower display, but Charlie did not see the funny side of his misfortune. Suddenly Fred and Charlie remembered Belvedere who, to their relief, was sitting amongst the many broken flower stems.

"You all right, Belvedere?" asked Fred and Charlie concerned that the landing might have hurt the little chap. Belvedere nodded that he was all right as he got to his feet and quickly ran to take cover under a bush. The many visitors to the Tower of London had now gathered to see what all the commotion had been about. Most had seen the landing and were laughing at Fred and Charlie who tried not to show their embarrassment.

As the crowd of spectators began to disperse, Fred and Charlie turned to the bush where Belvedere was now hiding and whispered.

" Sorry about the landing, we have to practise, but are you all right?" questioned Fred whilst Charlie kept watch. A Raven talking to a bush would attract even more attention than they already had.

"Yes, yes, I am all right, but you could have killed me. At least I can get home from here. Thank you for the lift, and do practise those landings. Oh, and good luck. I think you are going to need it," replied Belvedere. With a rustle of the bush the little travel companion of Fred and Charlie disappeared leaving the two brothers all alone to explore their new surroundings.

Looking around, Charlie noticed a plaque on the wall that they had very nearly hit during their landing and decided to investigate. Fred, not wanting to be left alone, followed his brother a little uneasily keeping a watchful eye.

"Ah right, yes. The Light Gower. Now this must be the building where that famous cricketer lives. I read about him in the Raven Press, you know. Does a lot of TV now with Garry Binacre, nice guy," explained Charlie with his chest all puffed out and an air of knowledge in his voice. What the plaque actually said was The White Tower, a very famous part of the Tower of London, but Fred did not have the heart to correct his brother as he always got things mixed up.

Just then Fred and Charlie nearly jumped out of their feathers as a voice boomed at them from the other side of the grass lawn. Fred and Charlie looked around not realising that the voice was in fact shouting at them. As the ferocious elder raven approached with wings a-flapping Fred and Charlie did not know whether to run or simply ignore him in the hope he might go away.

"Look what you have done. Years and years of work ruined, you young fools, whoever taught you to land like that? What have you got to say for yourselves?"

Fred and Charlie looked at each other in amazement. Who was this raven and why was he shouting at them so much? The grass was an accident after all and the flower-bed could be replaced. Charlie began to adjust his feathers and stepped forward holding a wing outstretched whilst holding Fred back with the other. Not that Fred was about to step forward.

"I'll handle this, Fred, don't worry. Probably that cricketer fellow. No problem. Probably his practice lawn we have landed on, a bit of a mess really, but I'll sort it out."

Fred had no intention of doing anything and simply raised his wing to his forehead as he knew Charlie was about to make a fool of himself again. Charlie lifted a wing to the finely dressed raven as if to say, "just hold on."

"Afternoon. Sorry about the grass, but we have been a fan of yours for many years now. I am sure you can get some grass seed and it will be fine in a few weeks or so and the flowers, well, they could be glued together. But at least now when you knock the ball into the borders you can see it. Any idea where we might find Hector, I think he might be a neighbour of yours!"

Fred could not believe his ears. One day Charlie would learn to keep his beak shut. The raven that stood before them was now very angry. In fact he was so angry he was lost for words for a brief time but finally he managed to gain his composure.

"Cricketer, Seed, The Odd Ball! You have ruined all my work

and all you can say is Cricketer, Seed, The Odd Ball. Do you know who I am?"

Fred and Charlie shook their heads, amazed at the further outburst of this finely dressed raven.

"I am Borderline, the famous raven gardener here at the Tower. I tend all the flowers and the lawns. No one walks on my lawns without permission. Neither does the Raven Master and he is human. I know who you are, the new recruits that Hector is expecting. Wait till he hears about this. You had better follow me and we shall see what he is going to do with you." With that Borderline turned on his claws and marched off towards a small tunnel opening next to some very old roman ruins. Fred and Charlie followed as instructed in silence listening to Borderline muttering under his breath. Every now and then Borderline would bend down and nudge a stone back into its rightful place with his beak.

Through the tunnel entrance they went down out of the sunshine into a series of dimly lit corridors passing the odd raven now and then. Still Borderline said nothing and kept muttering under his breath. Fred and Charlie felt very uneasy. Finally they reached a large old oak door, Borderline knocked and entered, but there was no one there.

"This is Hector's office. Wait here, he will be with you shortly and don't touch anything." Not giving Fred and Charlie the chance to answer Borderline marched off muttering about seeds and replanting flowers once again.

Hector's office was cold. It had a large desk that was cluttered with all sorts of books and feather pens. On one wall hung a very old map of London and a very badly painted picture of a raven hung on the other. Probably Hector, thought Fred. Charlie, however, was getting restless. The worst thing anyone could say to him was not to touch anything and he started to move from one foot to another.

"Stand still, Charlie, I think you have upset enough people without upsetting me," said Fred, still annoyed by his brother's outburst at Borderline.

"I have got cramp, that's all, anyway what sort of Chief Of Ravens calls his office OFFENCE? Did you see that sign on the door as we came in? I don't know. We crash land, get shouted at by a cricketer and pushed into a room and left I thin…" but Charlie did not have time to finish his sentence as the door suddenly burst open. Fred was sure that he saw Charlie gulp with fright, not that he would ever admit it.

Hector, dressed in his fine robes, walked behind his desk without saying a word and sat down. Placing a round pair of spectacles on the end of his beak, he opened a file that lay on his desk and began to read. Charlie did not say a word, much to Fred's relief, but began to scratch his beak with his wing tip.

"Stop that," said Hector without looking up from the file he was reading. Fred and Charlie looked at each other and raised their eyebrows as Hector grunted and turned the pages. At last Hector placed the file back on the desk, removed his spectacles and looked up at the two brothers.

"Bostrum's sons. Well, what a start you two have made, upsetting Borderline like that! We do have a landing strip in the old moat, you know. Not that it is used much now, but that is no excuse. Whatever would your father say? Never mind, we had better get down to business. An interesting file the two of you have." Hector got up from behind his desk and walked round to stand in front of Fred and Charlie. Smoothing out his robes Hector sat on the edge of his desk. "What are we going to do with you two?"

Charlie thought that Hector was not so scary now and decided to explain how sorry he and his brother were about the flowers and the grass, but Hector cut him off and continued to speak.

"Your Father has served at the Tower for many years and when he asked me to take on you two as recruits I knew that I could not say no. But whether you have the makings of Yeoman Raven Guards we shall have to see. Your Father has also asked me to read you a note that he left here for you last night."

Hector opened the envelope, pulled from it a piece of paper and began to read aloud. "Dear Fred and Charlie, Good luck, work hard and try to stay out of trouble. Listen to what Hector has to say. He is a very wise raven. Make me proud and I will see you in a few months. All the very best." Placing the paper back on the desk Hector turned once again to the two brothers. "So there you have it. Your father wishes you well and has left you in my care as he has now retired to the New Forrest. All it leaves me to do is to welcome you officially to the Tower of London as new recruits. So welcome."

Fred and Charlie seemed to be in a state of shock as neither of them uttered one word. Hector, now back behind his desk, pulled a piece of rope that hung from the ceiling before settling down to read a book he had selected from the many that were scattered across his desk. But before he opened it he once again addressed Fred and Charlie.

"Before you leave this office you must learn a little about the Tower of London and how it is important for you to take this job seriously. The White Tower, which you nearly crashed into on landing, was finished in 1097 AD. The Roman Wall that you flew over before crash landing has been here since the Dark Ages and the two inner walls were built sometime in the thirteenth century. Many humans have lost their lives here as well as many ravens. The old tales that surround this building also say that should the ravens leave the Tower of London the Monarchy will fall. In other words the King or Queen would not exist any more, and the tourists, Rucksacks as we call them would not come to visit. The Tower also holds dark secrets. The humans used to execute other humans here, and kings like Henry the Eighth had some of his wives', heads chopped off." Fred gulped at the very thought and Charlie was shaking from beak to claw, but still Hector continued.

"I have to say that a raven has never been executed here and during the disasters like the Great Fire Of London in 1666 AD we have always protected the buildings. Not one part of this building has ever been damaged by fire or even bombs from the Second World War, so you are really quite safe here. London has existed for many years. It was founded by the Romans and they called it Londinium after the great raven Londum. Oh, how I wish I had met with him, the hours of talking and learning would have been quite brilliant." Much to Fred and Charlie's relief there was a loud knock at the door. Although Hector's story was very interesting, he did go on a bit.

"Enter," shouted Hector.

Charlie whispered into Fred's ear as Hector chatted with the raven that had just entered the room. "This Hector's mad, you know, heads being cut off, kings and queens falling over. What have we let ourselves into? I don't know about you, Fred, but...." once again Charlie's sentence was cut short by Hector's rasping voice.

"Stop talking in the ranks." Hector sat with his wings tucked behind his head as he leant back in his old leather chair, a chair that had seen better days and looked like it might well collapse at any time. With a large yawn Hector introduced the raven that had just entered the room.

"This is Bascer, the tailor here at the Tower. He makes all of our beautiful uniforms." Fred and Charlie looked at each other, the last thing they would have said was that the uniforms were beautiful. They would have been quite happy to have been wearing their dungarees and Rike trainers, the most fashionable trainer for any up and coming raven.

"Bascer will take you and fit you with your new uniforms whilst I have, ooh, a little nap. Quite a long day it has been and I could do with a little sleep." Hector gave yet another one of his large yawns and stretched his wings, causing a few of his feathers to fall to the ground. Embarrassed at the loss of the feathers, Hector snatched them up and placed them in a jar on the window ledge with quite a few others that had obviously fallen out before.

"NOW GO," shouted Hector, irritated that Fred and Charlie should see him losing his feathers. The rumour around the Tower was that at night Hector could be seen in his office gluing them back into place, explained Bascer as he shut the door to Hector's office. Hector's office door flew open as soon as Bascer had shut it.

"And once they have got their uniforms made take them to Sledger and get him to train them." Once again the office door closed, this time to the sound of Hector muttering from within before the sound of snoring could be heard. Bascer leant against the wall in relief. Fred and Charlie watched as Bascer stood with his eyes closed for a few moments. Then, with a shake of his head, he turned to Fred and Charlie.

"Right, you two, we have a job to do and we have to make

these uniforms. Aha, the cost of all that material and oh dear, the cost of my time. Does no one appreciate around here how much things cost?" Fred and Charlie found it difficult to understand Bascer as he had a strange accent, but one that they found quite warming. As usual it was Charlie who spoke out first, much to the concern of his brother.

"Now, Bascer. May I call you Bascer? Yes, well that is how you were introduced so Bascer it is then. Look, we don't really have to wear these uniforms, do we? You see, Fred was only saying the other day that he would hate to wear a uniform. I am just looking after him, you know. After all blood is thicker than water. I do hope you understand." Charlie turned and smiled at his brother who curled his beak up at him. Bascer stopped in his tracks and turned to place his wings on Charlie's shoulders.

"My boy, of course you have to wear a uniform. We all have to wear a uniform and I really don't think that your brother said that, do you? In any case you can't guard tonight without a uniform, so we make the uniforms. They say it takes nine tailors to make a raven and I have two new recruits. Bessie, oh Bessie won't like this. She was hoping to go to her drama class this afternoon, but what can we do? Come on, let's get you two to the workshop." With that Bascer continued marching on. Charlie turned to his brother and once again said that they were all mad but Fred was not listening.

The corridors were very long and old. On each door they passed Fred and Charlie noticed name plates. Finally Bascer stopped at one particular door that read James Cromus Ravenous.

"The oldest Raven known to be alive. He is a hundred and forty years old, you know." explained Bascer pointing to the nameplate. Fred and Charlie tiptoed past the door so as not to wake the old raven. At last they stood in front of a door marked TAILOR.

"Here we are then, this is my workshop. Now, I don't want any rudeness in front of Bessie or she will take you in hand and you won't like that, I can assure you." Bascer turned the doorknob and opened the door and used his wing to guide Fred and Charlie in.

"I am home, dear. We have two new recruits to fit uniforms for. Where are you dear?" Bascer looked around the very full room. Bits of cloth hung on backs of chairs, and rolls of material were stacked on shelves from the floor to the ceiling. A large table filled the centre of the room and on it stood an old iron and a radio, which was on. Roono Rooks from Raven Radio at Tower Hill was playing the latest hits that echoed around the room.

Then, from under a pile of off cuts from uniforms, a Raveness appeared, with a tape measure round her neck and a pincushion pinned to her dress. Fred and Charlie knew that this had to be Bessie, Bascer's wife.

"I can hear you, Bascer, I can hear you, there is no need to shout is there? Now, what do we have here? Two New recruits eh. Oh look at those legs, aren't they thin? And those shoulders. Ugh, my, my. We will have to put some foam round them to fill them out a bit. Ah well, that's my drama class out of the window, so we had better get started. Okay, Bascer, you cut, I'll stitch, we should have this all done by teatime. Oh and I have just baked some fresh bagels so we can have them. Now come on, dear, chop chop, let's get to it." Bascer smacked his beak at the very thought of fresh bagels. Bessie made the best bagels for miles around, so the quicker the job was done the quicker the bagels could be served.

Fred and Charlie stood as still as they could whilst Bascer took their measurements. Charlie could not help chuckling as the tape measure tickled his sides, but Bascer ignored the young raven's outbursts and kept working.

Bessie and Bascer worked very quickly indeed. Red material flew about the room and the sound of snipping scissors echoed above the tunes on the radio. Fred and Charlie could not help but notice the stale smell of feathers and they both wondered how many uniforms had been made by Bascer and Bessie.

"Don't say much, do they, Bascer?" suddenly announced Bessie making Bascer cut off one of his feathers as he tried to shape a piece of material into a sleeve on his own wing.

"Oh, now look what you have made me do, I will be as bald as Hector by the time I leave this place," exclaimed Bascer as he continued his work, totally ignoring Bessie's original statement. Fred and Charlie for their first time in their lives had nothing to say. Perhaps it was the thought of their new uniforms or simply that they felt shy. For fear of seeming rude Charlie decided it was up to him to break the silence.

"Er..... so tell me, Bascer, what can you tell us about the Tower that Hector may have left out, that is of course if you are not too busy."

Bascer looked up at Bessie and winked. "Well, I see no reason why I can't tell you some of the horrors that have taken place here. Now, where shall I start. Ahhh Yes." As Bascer placed a thin piece of material over Charlie's left shoulder he began to tell his tales. Bessie, however, just kept working, only glancing over at Bascer from time to time when her husband's stories became a little unreal. Fred and Charlie thought that Bessie was keeping quiet because she had heard the stories so many times before which it has to be said was very true, but equally she did not want to encourage Bascer, not that he needed any encouragement. As he stitched he talked.

"Now then, there was the two ravens that got killed in World War Two. Hector never talks about that though. You see, my boys, one of the ravens that died was his brother, direct hit in the bird bath from a stray bomb. Booommm, up they went, never seen so many feathers in all my life. Then of course there was that German official that came to the Tower just after the war, cor deary me, got his boots pecked that day from Hector. Well you could not blame him, could you?" Fred and Charlie listened intently as Bascer went from tale to tale, only shaking their heads in agreement every now and then. Seeing that Bascer was enjoying himself so much and the new raven recruits were obviously engrossed, Bessie decided to slip off and reheat the bagels for their afternoon tea. But even from her kitchen she could hear Bascer chattering away.

"Now, what else can I tell you?" continued Bascer. "Ah yes, never take chewing gum from another raven. Big joke around here. You see, it is not chewing gum as you or I would know. No, it is putty from the windows, and BOY does it gum your beak up. Got caught once by it myself, cor deary me, it took weeks for me to be able to speak again."

Charlie suddenly let out a squawk as Bascer in all his excitement pricked him in the wing. Bascer didn't apologise but simply continued telling his tales about how the Tower was haunted at night. He told Fred and Charlie about the two brothers just like them, who had been imprisoned in the Devereux Tower many years ago. Now they can be found walking about at night with their heads in their hands as ghosts. If anyone should see them they would not recover from the shock, as they are such a terrible sight. The ghosts met their horrible death at the hands of the Executioner. Fred and Charlie were shaking from head to claw, but still Bascer pressed on.

"Well, it is like the time James Cromus Ravenous, the oldest raven — you know who I mean, we stopped outside his door. Now he has a few stories to tell like the time he met Anne

Boleyn — well, her ghost actually. She was walking around one night with her head under her arm. Henry the Eighth had her head cut off, you know, on that block stood out there. You will see it on guard duty tonight, mind you ..." Bascer leant forward so only Fred and Charlie could hear. "Like the time I saw one of those cannons out there smoking, smoking all on its own it was. Well, I said then, that's it. I am taking up tailoring and giving up guarding, safer in here away from all those ghosts."

"That's enough, Bascer, you will have these two scared out of their minds before they go out tonight," said Bessie who had returned with a large tray of bagels and tea.

"Proper little soldiers they are now, with those uniforms finished," said Bessie placing the tray on the table. Fred and Charlie looked at themselves in the long mirror that hung by the door. They looked just as their father had when he used to return home from a hard day's work.

"Wow, look at us, Charlie," shouted Fred. But Charlie was more interested in admiring himself in the mirror. A great big grin stretched from one end of his beak to the other. Bessie put the finishing touches, a tuck here and a tuck there. Then all was done. The uniforms were finished. Even though Fred and Charlie had not wanted their uniforms in the first place, they were so pleased that they could not help but look at themselves in the mirror.

Bascer explained that soon they had better find Sledger so

that he could complete his day's work and hand Fred and Charlie over so that they could begin their training as Yeoman guards. The news that they would soon begin their training brought Fred and Charlie to their senses and all of a sudden the great big grins on their beaks turned into unsure smiles.

Bessie wished Fred and Charlie well and told them to keep close to Bascer as they made their way down the corridors to where Sledger was. After Bascer's stories Fred and Charlie had no intention of leaving the tailor's side.

With a left here and a right there, Fred and Charlie found themselves once again on the lawn where they had caused so much damage earlier. Bascer pulled his collar up against the fine rain that had started to fall and, much to Fred and Charlie's concern, the sun was beginning to set. Soon it would be night.

Bascer pulled a matchbox from his coat pocket and took out a very strange-looking raincoat that was creased, having been squashed in the tiny matchbox. Fred and Charlie found it very hard not to laugh as Bascer put the raincoat on. He looked as if he was wrapped in cling film.

"Don't you two laugh at me. At least I will be dry although you two will become quite wet. Now, wait here until I get Sledger and stay away from Borderline."

As Bascer made his way to find Sledger, Fred and Charlie

noticed the silhouette of a raven amongst the flower-bed they had destroyed earlier. Borderline was still muttering to himself and the two brothers agreed with Bascer that the gardener was best left alone.

The misty drizzle soon began to soak through Fred and Charlie's new uniforms and as the sun sank out of sight a night chill ran down their spines. There was nobody about and it was only then that Fred and Charlie realised how scary the Tower could be even this early at night. It felt as if all the walls were watching them.

Fred rested his head on Charlie's shoulder much to his brother's unrest. Fred was never a affectionate brother. With each breath Fred took he beat his beak together making a very strange noise that unnerved Charlie a great deal.

"Stop that, Fred, stop messing around. Listen, I like these uniforms, you know. Perhaps I should go over and say a few words to Borderline?" But just as Charlie stepped forward Fred stopped him. Facing his brother Fred explained that perhaps he had better leave Borderline to his gardening. To Fred's surprise Charlie began beating Fred's beak with his wing, Fred immediately took a step back.

"What are you doing, Charlie?"

Charlie looked very sorry, and explained that he thought Fred's beak was on fire, but now realised that it was the cold night air making his breath come out like smoke. Fred accepted his brother's apologies, and not wanting to encourage his brother in beating his beak by talking, he decided to look around. He saw Bascer returning with another raven who must be Sledger.

" Ah now, then this must be Sledger. Now don't worry, Fred, I will deal with this. Got to get off to a good start with this Sledger character. I can talk to people in authority, you know, and I can read a lot better than you, Fred. Who knows, this Sledger may well have something for us to sign," explained Charlie once again puffing out his chest. Fred could not believe his brother sometimes, his uniform must have gone to his head. Suddenly Bascer and the other raven stopped, had a few words and then Bascer ran off without saying goodbye to Fred and Charlie. Charlie looked at Fred and Fred looked at Charlie as the raven that they hoped was Sledger approached. Fred whispered into Charlie's ear.

"Keep quiet, Charlie. I don't like the look of Sledger, he looks mean and what is that he is carrying?" But it was too late. Charlie had already stepped forward to greet Sledger, who was now standing with what looked like a rubber knife under his wing.

"Ah, Sledger. Now then, let me introduce my brother Fred, and I am Charlie. How about we go inside out of the rain and have a little chat about this training?" The raven seemed to get agitated at Charlie's gesture as Fred had expected.

" Sledger? Sledger? My Name Is Not Sledger. It is RIPPER,

and that is a name you will never forget," shouted the raven whose eyes seemed to glow red in the dark. As Ripper picked a seed from his beak with the rubber knife Fred and Charlie stepped back.

"So we have two new recruits. Now stand up straight and salute me on the double," ordered Ripper, watching Fred and Charlie fumbling to salute him. "I can see we are going to have some fun. Two new recruits with fresh feathers to pluck. Now turn to your left and march. LEFT, RIGHT, LEFT, RIGHT."

Marching was something Fred and Charlie had only played at when they were younger, and Charlie had not been very good then. The two young ravens tripped over each other's feet as they tried very hard to march in time. Ripper followed them shouting at the top of his voice. Then came the order to stop and Fred and Charlie bumped to a clumsy halt. The two brothers noticed that they had been joined by two other birds, but they were not ravens. Who could they possibly be, thought Fred and Charlie?

"Wait there, and no speaking in the ranks, do you understand," bellowed Ripper. Fred and Charlie had no intention of speaking at all but they could just hear what Ripper was saying as he greeted the two new arrivals.

"Sweeney, Todd, I told you never to come here, we arranged to meet at our usual spot later. Now what do you want?" said Ripper as he turned round to check Fred and Charlie were still there and not talking. Ripper huddled together with his friends and began to chat. Fred and Charlie could not hear what was being said, but Fred was certain he heard the words 'The Great London Adventure."

In no time at all Ripper had shaken the wings of his friends and as they flew off over the walls of the Tower Ripper returned to Fred and Charlie ordering them to march once again.

Soon Fred and Charlie were deep in the corridors of the Tower, but this time with no friendly faces to greet them — just the sound of Ripper's voice ordering them to march left and right. After what seemed to be an age Fred and Charlie found themselves outside yet another large door with a plaque on it. This time Fred read it aloud so there was no further confusion.

"The Waterloo Barracks Dining Hall."

Food at last, thought Charlie, who was beginning to feel a little hungry. At least this time Charlie understood the plaque. If he had read it, he would have probably read it as 'Bought A Loo With Carrots And A Climbing Broom', thought Fred.

Ripper pushed Fred and Charlie through the door into the room. Tables and chairs longer than Fred and Charlie had ever seen lined the walls and pictures hung above each table. The two brothers noticed that one of the pictures was of their father and they walked over to look at him in all his glory.

"Don't think your father can help you now, he is miles away. I'll pluck a few of his feathers the next time I see him."

Charlie had taken enough. He had never been spoken to the way he had since Ripper had arrived and now he had insulted his father. Charlie turned to face Ripper and curled up his beak. Fred took a deep breath in fear of what Charlie was going to do.

"What would you know? That picture is worth ten thousand words. Yes, he is our father and we are proud of it, so back off or we will pluck a few of your feathers." Fred was astonished at the bravery of Charlie. But Ripper was not impressed. He simply left the room laughing, shouting, "Don't move, I will be back."

"You fool, Charlie. What are you doing? That Ripper is nasty. I don't like him or trust him, so stop upsetting him," pleaded Fred as Ripper started shouting at someone else in the other room. Charlie did not have time to answer. The door that Ripper had left by suddenly burst open. This time Ripper was not alone, but the other raven looked a lot friendlier and was carrying a tray of food. As the other raven placed the tray on a table Ripper placed his rubber knife back into his belt and explained that this was Sledger. Ripper then stood in front of Charlie and banged his beak on Charlie's.

" As for you, I shall see you later."

Charlie wiped a bead of sweat from his brow, as Ripper

marched from the room swinging his rubber knife from side to side. Even Ripper's claws seemed to scratch the concrete as he walked and as the door slammed shut behind Ripper the three ravens let out sighs of relief.

"Cor blimey, hope he falls down the apples," said Sledger in a cockney accent.

"Apples? What Apples?" said Fred just as confused as Charlie.

"Apples and pears, you know, stairs. Cor, have you never heard of that before? Where have you been?" said Sledger beginning to dish out the food onto steel plates. Charlie shook his head in disbelief. He did not understand a word Sledger was saying. He was having enough problems with signs on the doors without learning a strange language. Sledger gestured to Fred and Charlie to take seats.

"Take the weight of your plates, me old Chinas."

"Plates?" questioned Fred again.

"Yes, yes. Plates of meat, your feet, cockney rhyming slang, you see, cor deary me, I can see we have a lot to learn, don't you?" explained Sledger. Fred and Charlie commented on how fresh the food was and Sledger told them how it was flown in fresh every day from markets all over London, markets like Smithfield. But the more Sledger talked the quicker he slipped back into talking his cockney rhyming slang until that is when he said about the frog and toad. At this point Fred and Charlie had to stop him.

"Hang on, Sledger. Frog and toad, we simply do not understand." questioned Fred, trying not to offend Sledger.

Sledger placed his head in his hands and banged his beak off the table.

"Okay. Look, a frog and toad is a road. See, it rhymes. Now then, a trouble and strife now that's your wife, a cockle and hen is ten, and your Harris well I think we will leave that for another day. You see I am a cockney, born within the sound of the Bow Bells at St Mary-le-Bow Church. And over the years us cockneys have spoken in slang, rhyming if you like, so that in the days when the gentry used to walk the streets of London they would not understand what we were saying. You will soon pick it up. I have a book I must lend you. It will teach you all the words." Sledger was right. Fred and Charlie were soon speaking the odd word or two of cockney by the end of their meal, much to the amusement of Sledger.

But they could not sit laughing and joking all night, there was training to be done. Sledger cleared the empty dishes with the help of Fred and Charlie and checked to see if the rain had stopped, which it had. So it was outside for the first night of Fred and Charlie's training.

Once outside in the courtyard and full up from their delicious meal Fred and Charlie took deep breaths, enjoying the fresh smell after rain as they always did. An orange glow filled the sky from the streetlights and the bright white moon glistened.

"Get on with your work, you three." boomed a voice, and as Fred, Charlie and Sledger looked up, Ripper was sitting on one of the roofs with his friends Sweeney and Todd, who were laughing so much they nearly fell.

"Just ignore them. How a second in command can behave like that I shall never know," said Sledger leading Fred and Charlie away. Once at a safe distance from the annoying influences of Ripper and his friends, Sledger began to explain Fred and Charlie's new job.

"Now look, Fred, Charlie. This job is very easy. All the buildings that surround you have names. The White Tower is over there, which I am sure the two of you remember very well. And that one is Wakefield Tower. That one is Salt Tower, and over there is Traitors' Gate, that is where they used to row the prisoners in from the Thames. Next to it is the Bloody Tower where the prisoners were kept, sometimes for years upon end. That is one place you don't want to guard at night, but for now all you have to do is walk about and check that the doors are all locked. Simple, you see. Now follow me." Sledger walked across the lawn that was kept so very well — probably by Borderline, thought Fred — and stopped by a large wooden block.

"Now this here is the old chopping block. This is where they used to chop off the heads of all the prisoners many years ago." Sledger looked about and with a wave of his wing Fred and Charlie drew closer. Sledger carried on with his tale but this time in a whisper.

"According to old raven tales, on the night of the fifth of December if a raven sits upon this block all his feathers will fall out, so no one ever sits on the block. They say that the brave ones that have dared to sit on it have been known to get very large splinters, and that is where the saying comes from 'A Chip Off The Old Block'. So bear that in mind."

Just then the tower clock struck one o'clock and startled the two brothers and Sledger. Fred and Charlie had never before stayed up this late. What an adventure they were having so far. Sledger, however, seemed to panic as the clock chimed its final chime.

"Oh dear, Oh dear, I am late. What am I to do? She will be sure to tell me off. Look, check all the doors are locked as I have to go somewhere for a short while. And stay away from Ripper and his friends. If they should turn up, squawk at the tops of your voices and I shall return." With that Sledger was gone leaving Fred and Charlie all alone and not giving them any chance to ask any questions.

"What is it with all these ravens, Fred? They keep leaving us. I am going to have to report this to Hector if it continues."
"Oh, shut up, Charlie. He said he will be back and so he will. Come on, let's check a few doors and stick close by just in case," said Fred, a little angry with his brother.

"In case of what?" whispered Charlie, but Fred was not listening. After a short while of checking doors, Fred and Charlie decided to take a rest by a very large bush giving them plenty of cover from Ripper who was still sitting on the roof talking to Sweeney and Todd. It was here that Fred and Charlie heard a strange noise. Then all of a sudden something bounced off Fred's beak.

"Did you see that, Charlie? What was it?"

"It's Ripper spitting those seeds at us. Where is he? He has come for me, Fred. I am going to be bald. Don't let him make me bald, please, Fred. I will never open my beak again, I promise."

Charlie clung to Fred, shaking so much that his buttons on his uniform rattled. Then all of a sudden Fred and Charlie heard their names being called. Looking about with great care the two brothers noticed Belvedere sitting in the bush behind them. He had been using a rolled up leaf as a peashooter and seeds from the lupins as ammunition. With one last deep breath Belvedere let out a high-pitched note to ensure Fred and Charlie had heard him. So strong was the note that Belvedere fell from his branch.

Fred and Charlie helped Belvedere back onto his branch and as they did so gold dust sprinkled to the floor. It was at this point that Fred and Charlie's life as they knew it was about to change.

2
chapter

The great meeting

Belvedere, who had regained his posture after his fall and disposed of his rolled leaf, rustled the bush once again to attract the attention of Fred and Charlie, who were keeping a keen eye out for Ripper just in case he should turn up and spot their little friend.

"I bet you were wondering why I have come to see you so soon," said Belvedere who was sitting on a branch swinging his legs back and forth as if he were sitting on a swing.

"Well, when I got home The Great Gob himself asked to see me. I thought he was going to keep me in for a few weeks as punishment, but, even so, to be stood in front of the Great Gob was such an honour. Anyway he wanted to know how I had returned home safely in daylight, so I explained how you had helped me with the lift, even if the landing was a bit rough and how kind you had been."

Fred and Charlie moved in closer to the bush so they could hear Belvedere more clearly. If anyone was to find them talking to a bush now they would be sure to be placed in one of the towers forever and everyone would be told that they were the mad ravens, but nevertheless as Belvedere continued with his story Fred and Charlie listened intently.

"So there I was listening to The Great Gob and you will never guess what he told me!"

"What?" said Fred and Charlie together.

"He wants to meet us, all three of us together, tonight. I am telling you there could be a medal in this for you and fresh cinnamon sticks for me."

Fresh cinnamon sticks. Charlie shuddered at the very thought. But Fred, being as practical as ever, pointed out that they could not leave the Tower on their first night. Poor Sledger would be worried out of his mind and if Ripper heard that he had lost his two new recruits Sledger would be sure to be plucked of his every feather.

"No, no, you don't understand. The Great Gob will make sure that Hector knows where you are and there will be no trouble for you or this Sledger chap. Don't worry, it will be fine. Now come on. We have to leave now," said Belvedere being as persuasive as possible. That was all Charlie needed to know; he was ready to follow the little Gronk anywhere. Now all he had to do was convince his brother that it would be fine.

"There you are, Fred. The Great Gob will send word to Hector, so Sledger will be alright and we get to meet the Ruler of all the animals in London. Ah, what a chapter for my book when I write it."

Fred rolled his eyes and reluctantly agreed to go. Just then, however, Fred and Charlie heard someone whistling behind them. Belvedere ducked out of sight and the two brothers looked up at the night sky.

"Wonderful evening, Fred, just wonderful. That Patrick Core would be so impressed. Well known in the world of glittery things in the sky, he is you know." Fred nodded his head in agreement not wishing to blow Charlie's diversionary discussion and as Charlie muttered on about the sparkly things being in shapes like a plough and a great bear, a Yeoman Raven Guard who they had never seen before walked past.

"What are you two meant to be doing, guarding the Tower? HA HA HA. Let's see what the Raven Master has to say about this. Can't have you watching the skys when you should be checking for our safety, youngsters!" said the Yeoman Guard shaking his head as he walked off.

"Is the coast clear?" Asked Belvedere poking his head out from the shelter of the bush.

"Yes, all clear, but if we are going to leave, we have to leave now. He has gone to get the Raven Master whoever he is, and that surely means trouble, so come on, let's go," spluttered Charlie who was all excited about meeting the Great Gob and setting off on yet another adventure. Fred was still not convinced and once again tried to persuade his brother not to go. It was no use, however, and with a shake of their feathers Fred and Charlie followed Belvedere into the bushes, which was not as easy for them as the little Gronk was far smaller than they were.

As the last tail feather of Fred and Charlie disappeared out of sight, Sledger appeared at the door he had entered some time before. Walking across the vast lawns of the Tower including the one that required a lot of repair Sledger looked about for his two trainee recruits, but there was no sign of them.

Poor Sledger began to panic as he looked high and low for Fred and Charlie. Sledger was convinced that Ripper probably had them and was plucking feathers out as he searched. If only he had not left them to go and see his girlfriend Janous! Fred and Charlie were sure to be bald by now and Hector would certainly send him to the claw-polishing department.

By this time Sledger was beside himself and he sat down with his head in his hands, when all of a sudden he noticed a pile of gold dust sparkling on the floor to the right of his foot. Sledger got to his feet and approached the gold dust with great care. He had never seen anything like this before.

The brilliant gold dust was too much of a temptation for Sledger and so he stuck his beak right in the middle of the pile and took a large sniff. Which was really a silly thing to do. With a large sneeze Sledger sat back with a start, then gave another big sneeze and another as he tried to catch his breath. Finally the sneezing stopped and to Sledger's horror his beak was glowing a brilliant gold.

"What is it, what is it? Oh, please someone help me. I will be a good raven for the rest of my life, I promise," shouted Sledger at the top of his voice as he ran round in a circle. Sledger tried to rub his beak clean with his wings only to discover that his wings were now covered in the gold dust.

"It is radiation. I am doomed," shrilled Sledger. He had heard some of the Rucksacks (tourists) talking about radiation once as they walked about the Tower and they had said that it glowed just like his beak and now his wings. Suddenly Sledger thought of Janous. She would never marry him if his beak fell off. After all, how would they kiss?

Sitting down once again, Sledger collected his thoughts. He knew that he needed help. He couldn't go to Hector. He would be sure to put him on claw polishing and demote him for losing Fred and Charlie. That only left one other raven he could go to and that was Ripper. Sledger gulped at the very thought. He was bound to lose a few feathers. But, worst of all, he could be in Ripper's debt for the rest of his life. Sad at the prospect of meeting Ripper, Sledger got to his feet, almost forgetting all about the gold dust that covered his beak and wing.

Fred and Charlie had no idea how much distress Sledger was in, but they had heard his cries, as half of London must have. Undisturbed, the two brothers headed through a hole Belvedere had found by Traitors' Gate. They turned round to take one last look at the Tower before they left with Belvedere. Fred and Charlie suddenly noticed Sledger walking across a large courtyard looking very sad and his beak and wing sparkled from the moon rays bouncing off the gold dust.

"Is Sledger going to be alright with all that gold dust on him? He doesn't look happy at all," questioned Fred who felt that they should have left a note or something.

"Yes, he will be fine. His beak may fall off but that is all," chuckled Belvedere. Fred and Charlie stopped in their tracks, first of all checking themselves and then watching Sledger.

"I am only joking. Cor, you two are so easy to tease. Gold dust brings you good luck as well as bringing a sparkle into your life. So don't worry. Sledger will be fine. Trust me, I am a Gronkiedoddle."

Happy that Sledger was not in any danger, Fred and Charlie continued to follow the little Gronk. Traitors' Gate was a spooky place and Fred and Charlie had not forgotten Bascer's tales of how people had been imprisoned and died there. Strange noises echoed off the walls and the two brothers kept very close to Belvedere. Charlie could not be certain, but he was sure that someone or something was watching them. Much to Charlie's delight and in no time at all the three of them were standing on a cobbled street. One more set of gates and Fred, Charlie and Belvedere were free to meet The Great Gob. Belvedere edged his way along the wall telling Fred and

Charlie to keep close and to keep in the shadows as human guards kept guard from the sentry box that lay ahead. Fred and Charlie did as they were told.

On tiptoe, inch by inch, the three of them edged their way along the wall trying not to make a sound. As they passed the sentry box they could hear the guard snoring. Charlie raised his wing.

"SHHHHSHHH." Charlie did like to think that he was in charge, thought Fred as they slowly crept past the snoring guard. Once at the final set of gates Belvedere whispered and told his travelling companions that they had to squeeze through the bars of the gate.

Charlie, being the largest, went first. With his beak in the air and trying very hard to make himself smaller he squeezed himself through. Suddenly there was a muffled squawk from Charlie.

"Fred, I am stuck."

"Breathe in, Charlie, breathe in," whispered Fred, concerned that the snoring guard might wake. With all their might Fred and Belvedere pushed until finally Charlie shot through the gates and skidded across the street before coming to rest by a parked car. Fred and Belvedere rolled about the floor in fits of laughter, totally forgetting about the snoring guard.

"Halt, who goes there," boomed the voice of the guard who

had awoken from his sleep with all the commotion. Fred and Belvedere shot through the gates and to safety on the other side. They were outside the Tower. Why had they not flown, thought Fred and Charlie, but Belvedere had not wanted to risk another bad landing and flying would have attracted too much attention.

Their uniforms muddy, Fred and Charlie looked at each other. They had looked so fine just a short while ago, but now they looked as if they had been dragged through a hedge backwards.

With no time to spare Belvedere quickly moved Fred and Charlie on to their destination, the meeting place of The Great Gob.

Back at the Tower Sledger was still in a terrible state. En route to Ripper, Sledger had not seen a piece of chewing gum that had been dropped on the ground earlier that day. Within minutes Sledger was tangled up in the chewing gum. Strands of gum clung to his feathers like glue and it took him quite some time to escape from the gum's grip.

Once free Sledger looked himself up and down. He could not believe the mess he was in.

"All the bars of soap in China will not get this lot cleaned up," muttered Sledger who was now tired and very worried that his beak might fall off at any time. With the very last drop of energy Sledger took to the rooftops to find Ripper. Sledger's glowing beak meant that he found it very difficult to judge the distance in front of him and as a result of this he landed with a bang right on his glowing beak.

As Sledger slid down the roof the sound of his scraping claws echoed around the Tower. The roof, still wet from the earlier rain, was too slippery to get a grip on and finally Sledger came to an abrupt stop in the guttering.

Soaking wet and now with a bent beak, Sledger hoped that he had not gone through all this trouble in vain only for Ripper to have gone out with Sweeney and Todd. Dropping down onto a window ledge Sledger peered through the window and, sure enough, saw Ripper asleep in a large silver bowl on a large oak table.

Ripper looked very funny with his tongue hanging out of his beak and snoring away, but Sledger knew that when he woke up he would be even more grumpy than usual. Then again what choice did Sledger have?

With an air of hesitation Sledger slid open the window and flew over to the table where Ripper was sleeping. Smiling to himself Sledger noticed Ripper's leg that was dangling over the edge of the silver bowl. Not able to resist the temptation, Sledger tickled Ripper's leg with his feathers.

First one eye then the other opened and Ripper yawned and stretched with all his might. Suddenly Ripper noticed Sledger and leaned forward to take a sleepy look just to be sure, thinking that he might still be dreaming. As the image before him cleared, Ripper let out a loud squawk.

"I'll never pull another feather, don't hurt me, whoever you are."

Ripper's sudden outburst made Sledger jump, which in turn made Ripper jump causing him to fall out of his bowl. Shielding his eyes from Sledger's bent beak, Ripper continued to mutter about how sorry he was and how he would never pluck another feather for the rest of his life, but as Ripper lowered his wing an evil glare took over his face.

"SLEDGER," shouted Ripper who bent down, picked up a lace napkin, and threw it over Sledger's beak. "There that should save the eyes from all that glow coming from your beak." Sledger backed away as Ripper edged his way towards him.

"Now then, Sledger, gold dust all over you, a bent beak. You have seen one of those Gronkiedoddles, have you not? Now tell me where their tunnel is? I need to know, you hear me? I need to know."

Sledger had no idea what had come over Ripper. He had never seen him like this before and as Ripper's breath snorted down at him through his beak Sledger felt a bead of sweat fall from his brow.

Fred and Charlie had no idea that Ripper had Sledger in his grasp and was being interrogated by him. They were more interested in their meeting with The Great Gob. Belvedere had led the two brothers to a jetty under a very tall bridge by the River Thames and told them that all they had to do now was wait.

The jetty was cold, wet and badly lit. The sound of dripping water echoed loudly and the lapping of the Thames against its banks seemed never to stop. Fred and Charlie could just about make out what the little Gronk was saying as he paced up and down.

"This is the place where we are to meet The Great Gob. You must never tell anyone about this place, never. Now, so you don't get bored I thought I would tell you a little about the bridge we are standing under."

Fred and Charlie settled down on the many steps that formed a small amphitheater going down to the water's edge whilst Belvedere marched up and down with his arms waving about and pointing to the bridge above.

"The bridge that stands high above us is, of course, Tower Bridge. Work began on the bridge in 1866 and it was opened on the 30th of June, 1894," explained Belvedere who by now was finding it very hard to keep Fred and Charlie's attention. The two brothers thought Belvedere's chat was very interesting, but they were very impatient to meet The Great Gob. Finally Belvedere suggested that they get some rest. Fred and Charlie cleaned themselves up and Belvedere sat reading a comic on an old mooring post.

Sledger, however, was not so comfortable. Ripper had him pinned up against the wall and had already plucked quite a few feathers which he hoped to sell onto Hector later.

"Now tell me where the Gronkiedoddle is, and where the tunnels are, Sledger (pluck). I know you know (pluck) and I know you know I know (pluck). I will send you to the London Dungeon over the water if you don't tell me (pluck). One place you don't want to go, Sledger (pluck). Now TELL ME."

Sledger cried in pain as another feather was plucked from his legs. Poor Sledger's legs were looking quite bare by now. The London Dungeon where Ripper was threatening to send him was a place Sledger had heard about. People and ravens entered, but no one had ever been seen to leave.

Just then a rattle from the window disrupted Ripper's plucking session and as he turned round the huge shape of Hector could be seen silhouetted against the bright moon.

"THAT'S ENOUGH, RIPPER," shouted Hector at the top of his voice. Ripper immediately started to brush Sledger down whilst trying to kick the plucked feathers out of sight. Ripper knew this time he had been caught red-handed and could not explain his actions as fun.

Hector flew down to join Ripper and Sledger and on landing knocked Ripper clean out of the way and sent him skidding along the floor on his bottom. With each foot that Ripper travelled more and more splinters collected in his bottom, a very painful experience.

Uninterested in Ripper's squeals of pain, Hector offered Sledger a steady wing for support. Ripper collected himself together in the corner and was looking at his bottom that now was full of splinters. Looking up he noticed that Hector was now staring at him. Hector's face spoke a thousand words. Never had Ripper seen him so angry and his voice seemed to boom at him from all corners of the room.

"Much noise has disturbed me tonight. Shouts from the dark concern me, I have heard bad things about you, Ripper, but this is not acceptable. I will not tolerate bullying in any shape or form, it is the most cowardly thing I know. This will not go unpunished."

Ripper hung his head low in shame whilst Hector brought a chair over for Sledger to rest upon. As Hector began to check over Sledger Ripper muttered and pulled splinters from his bottom. Sledger was confused that Hector had not mentioned his beak or the gold dust, but the time had come for him to tell Hector that he had lost Fred and Charlie.

"Sir, I have something to tell you -"

But Hector was not listening. "Now let's have a look at you. The feathers on your legs will grow back. That beak will need a bit of work to be straightened and you might look like a boxer for a while but never mind. And the gold dust will soon be gone. Now where did you get the gold dust?"

Sledger explained to Hector all about the gold dust and Fred and Charlie going missing and how he had crashed into the roof. He left out the bit about the chewing gum as he felt that Hector might think him a little stupid, but he told him how he had come to Ripper as second in command for help and the rest he could see for himself.

"Don't worry about the gold dust, Sledger, that will soon go. In any case it is to bring happiness, so you should be happy. And I will explain all about the Gronkiedoddles later. Now I think you should go to that girlfriend of yours and get some plasters. As far as Fred and Charlie are concerned, only time will tell and we shall have to wait and see, but if they are with a Gronkiedoddle then no harm will come to them so don't worry." Hector suddenly stopped and turned round to catch Ripper pulling faces at him behind his back. "That's it, Ripper, I have had enough of you. You can't even sit there and be trusted to behave. You just can't keep that beak of yours out of trouble." Ripper gulped and tried to hide his fear, but Hector continued to shout. "I think I will send you to the tar dump where Jackie and Eugene are. Six years should do it. They have been there for four years now. I sent them there for attacking Rucksacks (humans). You are a bully and I hate bullies."

Hector looked as if he was going to burst with anger and Ripper cried and pleaded not to be sent to the tar dump in Wales. Everyone knew about the tar dump. All you did was shovel tar day in and day out and you could never get the smell out of your feathers.

With a crisp order Hector told Ripper to gather all the ravens by the White Tower as they needed a council meeting to know what to do. Without hesitation Ripper flew out of the window. Once outside Ripper looked back as Hector once again began to help Sledger. An evil grin spread across his face. Before he gathered everyone together he would see Sweeney and Todd at the London Dungeon. He would get even with Sledger, Fred and Charlie for all the trouble they had caused.

Hector gathered Sledger together and reassured him that he would soon be back to his old self. And then the two of them flew off to the Raven Hospital. In the meantime Ripper had spread the word about the meeting. No one had dared ask Ripper about his splintered bottom and once the last raven had been told about the meeting Ripper headed out over the Thames to visit Sweeney and Todd.

Over the Thames Ripper flew. Below him H.M.S Belfast was moored. Through one of the small portholes a light flickered. Professor Admiral Naffi was working late on one of his mad inventions. The old ship's cat was out on deck with his paws in his ear waiting for another explosion. Ripper wondered what the mad professor was working on this time. Some years ago he carpeted the famous aircraft carrier's decks so all the jets could land in comfort but as the jets took off from the runway their jet engines set fire to the carpet and a near disaster happened.

Onward Ripper flew as fast as he could, taking a brief second to admire himself in one of windows of a large office building before finally coming to rest on the roof of the London Dungeon where Sweeney was taking a nap.

"Ripper, what are you doing here? You never said that you were going to pop over. Todd is down in the dungeon. Fancy a cup of boiled worms? They are very fresh this time of year," said Sweeney getting to his feet to greet Ripper properly. Ripper accepted the offer of boiled worms and followed Sweeney to an air vent in the roof. Banging his foot Sweeney called the lift that turned out to be an old pie tin and did not look very safe at all.

"It's quite safe, Ripper. We use it all the time, just hang on tight," explained Sweeney who had noticed Ripper's concerned look. Hopping on, Ripper clung to Sweeney for support and in a matter of seconds the pie tin vanished down the air vent.

All that could be heard as the pie tin plummeted down were the cries from Ripper until it finally came to rest amongst wax models of humans that were sitting around a table.

Asign in the middle of the middle of the table read 'The Table Of Henry the Eighth'. Ripper had heard all about this king and how he had chopped some of his wives' heads off. Ripper gulped at the very thought.

Sweeney hopped off the tin and told Ripper to follow him and to keep close. But Ripper's landing on the table was not as he had expected, a claw on his right foot caught the large plate

of food that was in front of the king and to the horror of
Ripper the king let out a loud belch. This sent Ripper flapping
across the table in fright much to Sweeney's delight.

"Come on, Ripper, don't let Henry there bother you. There are
plenty of other things in here that will make your feathers
stand on end."

Not allowing time for Ripper to gain any form of confidence,
Sweeney took off into the darkness. Ripper, who suddenly felt
very alone, took after Sweeney. This way and that Ripper
followed Sweeney and the strange noises he kept hearing
hurried him along. Ripper was convinced that by the time he
caught up with Sweeney all his feathers were going to be
white with fright.

Just then as Ripper turned yet another dark corner a head
appeared and seemed to float in the air. Ripper froze, his beak
chattered with fright as the head spoke to him.

"Hello Ripper, welcome to the London Dungeon. I had my
head chopped off where you live. I do hope we can talk later.
I bet the Tower has changed since I was there."

Ripper's eyes stood out on stalks, and as the head vanished
as quick as it had appeared Ripper heard another noise to the
right of where he was standing.

"Booo!" shouted Sweeney. This was all too much for Ripper,
and he shot off into the dark.

"Ripper, it is only me!" Shouted Sweeney, but Ripper was not listening or hanging around to listen to Sweeney. Eventually when Sweeney caught up with Ripper he was crouched in a corner with his beak chattering away with fright. After a short time Sweeney had reassured Ripper that he was safe and suggested that they went to see Todd who was in the coffee shop.

Todd was surprised to see Ripper as he looked up from his newspaper, The Horror Gazette. Todd made Ripper feel welcome by offering him the best seat in the coffee shop. Ripper, who was still in a state of shock, sat on a seat next to Todd at the coffee bar and it was then that he noticed three heads on silver trays. Sweeney placed a mug of hot boiling worms in front of Ripper who was staring at the heads. This London Dungeon was a terrible place to live, thought Ripper, as he tried to ignore the heads, but then, to Ripper's horror, one of the heads spoke to him.

"We know what's wrong with you. You are scared out of your wits."

The other two heads agreed and started to laugh aloud, making their trays rattle. Todd told Ripper to relax and introduced him to the three heads.

"These are Christie, Crippen, and Moriarty, three friends of ours. Well, parts of friends."

Everyone once again began to laugh at Todd's attempt at a

joke, but Ripper could not see the funny side. Although Ripper did not feel as scared, he was very apprehensive of the three heads.

"How can you live here with all these awful things around you? I mean to say kings that belch, heads that talk and I saw Dracula flying about."

Sweeney explained that Henry the Eighth belched as he always did to let them know someone was coming and the others were their friends that just stayed there. The London Dungeon was their home. As for the three heads, well, they just kept them company at night.

Ripper was not convinced, but with all the laughter and okes at his expense out of the way, he explained how he had been caught by Hector plucking Sledger's feathers and that Hector was now considering sending him to the tar dump in Wales. Sweeney and Todd could never allow their friend to be sent to Wales and offered Ripper a bed at the Dungeon. He would have to live in exile there. Ripper declined the offer rather hastily.

Looking about, Ripper, in a quiet but sinister voice told his two friends of how he intended to plead with Hector to let him stay so that he was at the Tower when the Gronkiedoddle returned with Fred and Charlie. Then he was going to kidnap the Gronkiedoddle and insist that he take him to the tunnels where he lived. Once he knew where the tunnels were he could then demand in return for the safety of the

Gronkiedoddle the great book that contained all the secrets of London and where much of the great wealth was stored. The book Ripper was talking about was The Great London Adventure, a book only the Grand Master and The Great Gob had access to.

With the book safely in his hands he would take over from Hector and live in luxury at the Tower from the wealth of the hidden fortunes the great book would lead him to.

Asmile beamed across Ripper's face at the thought of making Hector clean his claws and Sweeney and Todd could see themselves ordering Sledger to clean the Dungeons. What fun that would be!

A loud cheer rang out from the three birds and even Crippen, Christie and Moriarty joined in.

"But first we have to capture that Gronkiedoddle," said Ripper gaining everyone's attention once again.

"Once I get back to the Tower I will know if my pleading with Hector will work. If it does, I shall wait for the Gronkiedoddle to turn up. Then I shall grab him and bring him here and I want you two to deal with Fred and Charlie, tie them up and hide them somewhere. We will deal with them later!"

Sweeney and Todd agreed with Ripper's plans. At last his troops were coming together and soon he would have all he needed to rule over everyone at the Tower.

Ripper left the dungeons with Sweeney and Todd at his side and felt a little more at ease except when Anne Boleyn expressed her best wishes. As he did not wish to hang around Ripper quickened his pace.

Once at the pie tin lift Henry the Eighth belched once again and before Ripper knew where he was he was back up on top of the roof. With his plans now set and Sweeney and Todd waving goodbye, Ripper took to the air and felt a sense of power as he looked over London. One day it would all be his to rule.

H.M.S Belfast shook below as yet another explosion took place and sparks showered the Thames. Professor Naffi and the two ship's cats, Cleo and Frankenstein, staggered from a doorway.

"It's alright, Cleo, Frankenstein. I will change the charge. Next time the inflatable hammock will open without a hitch."

But the two cats were not waiting around to find out and scurried down the ship's decks before disappearing down one of the large gun turrets. Ripper could not help but chuckle at the spectacle down below. The night air began to chill and Ripper's bottom was beginning to get sore now, so he decided to head back to the Tower for Hector's meeting before he caught a cold.

Ripper landed safely at the Tower and made his way through the crowd of ravens that had now gathered. No one had noticed that he had been away, but he was conscious of all the chuckles amongst the ravens as he made his way to the front of the crowd. They were obviously laughing at his splintered bottom but all he could do was to curl his beak and mutter to himself.

Suddenly silence fell as Hector entered the courtyard from the Hospital door followed closely by Sledger whose legs and beak had been carefully bandaged. Even Primous, an older raven that never stopped grooming himself, left his feathers alone as he stared in amazement. As muttering spread amongst the gathered ravens, Hector raised his wings.

"SILENCE."

Hector turned to Ripper and told him to stand on one leg, which, needless to say, caused yet another ripple of muttering. Hector stood with his beak pointed to the sky gathering his thoughts and everyone wondered why Sledger was covered in bandages and why Ripper had splinters in his bottom. At last Hector took a deep breath and addressed his fellow ravens.

"Tonight is a sad night for us all. I have found out that a trusted member of our community has been bullying. The raven I talk about is RIPPER." With a wing outstretched Hector pointed at Ripper who hung his head in shame as all the Ravens looked at him in disgust. Once again Hector's voice silenced the crowd. "And, by order of the Raven Realm, I here by demote him from the position of Second In

Command to Private Ripper. He will join you on your nightly duties and during the day I will set him special duties of work. I will not tolerate bullying in any shape or form. I wish to hear if this excuse for a raven even lifts a wing in the wrong way and, if he does, he will be sent to the tar dump in Wales."

A loud cheer rang out. Ripper had subjected many of the ravens to his bullying and now justice had been served and Ripper finally had been caught. For Ripper this was worse than being sent to Wales as he was going to have to watch his back now. Once again Hector raised his wing and the crowd settled.

"Now to more important things. Two new recruits have gone missing. I believe that they have left with a Gronkiedoddle. For those of you that have not heard of the Gronkiedoddles they are little men that live under this great City with The Great Gob, the Ruler and Master of all the animals."

With that all the ravens let out a loud cheer. "The Great Gob, Ruler and Master of all the animals."

"I want you all to keep a keen eye out for Fred and Charlie, the two new recruits. I am sure their disappearance has something to do with the great book 'The Great London Adventure'. But we will not know until they return. Now return to your posts. Daylight is nearly upon us and we have to get ready for another day of visiting Rucksacks (tourists). Sledger, Ripper and Sybulus I want to see you in my office

61

now." With that Hector hopped off the orange box that he had been using so all could see him and marched off leaving the guards to talk amongst themselves. A few of them made noises at Ripper and stuck their tongues out at him, knowing he could do nothing to hurt them.

As Sybulus, Sledger and Ripper made their way to Hector's office, Ripper noticed that Sweeney and Todd were sitting on the roof of the Tower and wondered if they had heard him being demoted from Second In Command. Perhaps they would not be his friends any more, thought Ripper, as he entered the corridor that led to Hector's office. Once inside the quiet corridors, Ripper seized the chance to have a word with Sledger.

"I want to know where those tunnels are, Sledger, and if you don't tell me I shall pluck the rest of your feathers out."

But Sledger was not listening. He knew that if Ripper touched him he would be sent to Wales, but just to be safe Sledger quickened his step. As the three ravens arrived at Hector's office they noticed the door was wide open and Hector was sitting behind his desk cleaning his claws with a pipe cleaner, something he always did when he was angry. Hector called the three of them in.

Ripper, Sledger and Sybulus stood before Hector who was now reading a file. After a short while Hector placed the file down on the desk. The atmosphere in the room was very tense and, as Hector rose and walked over to the map of

London on the wall, he began to speak.

"Right, Sybulus, you are a very wise traveller. I want you to go down to the New Forrest and find Bostrum, Fred and Charlie's father. Explain to him that it is of the utmost importance that he comes to see me. Now go, and hurry."

Sybulus saluted Hector, turned on his claws and marched from the office. Hector cleared his throat and placed his spectacles on the end of his beak.

"I am disgusted with you, Ripper. This is your last chance to prove that you can behave in a sensible fashion to others. I have decided that during the day you will clean roofs and sweep the courtyards. You will rest between three and six in the afternoon, then you will be on duty as a guard for the rest of the time. If I hear of you bullying once, it is the Tar Dump for you. After six months I shall review your position, but you will never be Second In Command again. Do you understand?" Ripper nodded politely, agreeing with Hector.

"Now, get out and get on with cleaning the roofs. I shall inspect them later," shouted Hector. Ripper left the office without a word. Clean roofs, he thought to himself. He was going to see Sweeney and Todd and find this Gronk, that's what he was going to do, thought Ripper, as he ambled his way back through the corridor. Then, just as he passed a suit of armour that had once belonged to Henry the Eighth, the armour spoke to Ripper.

"You have seen ANNE, Ripper!" Ripper fled from the corridor and did not stop running until he was safely outside.

Back in Hector's office Hector offered Sledger a seat, realising that his legs were obviously causing him some pain. As Hector tapped his beak with his letter opener he pondered what to do with Sledger. Finally he placed the letter opener on the desk and sat down himself.

"I have been thinking what to do with you, Sledger! In one night you have been bullied, but still you left your post to see Janous, not a very clever thing to do. I have learnt of your love for Janous and how much she means to you. So I have decided to make you Second In Command, but you will have to declare your love for Janous openly and I think you two should be married. With this position comes great responsibility and I hope you are mature enough to act in a professional way when your honour is at stake."

Sledger agreed and told Hector that he felt certain he could do the job. Just then there was a tap at the door and Hector in his usual way shouted, "Enter."

The door opened and, to Sledger's surprise, Janous walked in. Hector showed Janous to a seat and began to explain how he was making Sledger Second In Command. He also explained how he did not want any more scuttling around in the dark meeting secretly and that their love for each other had to be out in the open. Janous agreed and told Hector how she had a lot of faith in Sledger. She was certain that he would do a good job. Hector listened with great interest and finally asked Sledger if he had anything to say.

Sledger took Janous by the wing and knelt before her, Janous fluttered her eyelashes, slightly embarrassed, as Sledger asked her to marry him. Janous accepted and Sledger suddenly panicked. He had no ring to place on her wing. Hector, however, had already thought of this and offered Sledger a beautiful, glistening ring.

"This ring belonged to my wife and when she died I had it removed. I would be happy for you two to have it and I hope it brings you as much happiness as it did for my wife and me."

Janous wiped away a tear from her beak and Sledger thanked Hector with all his heart. Looking deep into Janous's eyes, Sledger placed the ring on her wing. Hector blew his nose, obviously touched by the scene before him. But they had to get back to business and, as Hector gave one last blast on his beak and cleared his throat, he continued.

"Good. Now it is official you are to be married, I will make the arrangements for the wedding. Now I had better make it official and swear you in as Second In Command." Hector lifted a sword from the side of his desk and placed it on Sledger's shoulders.

"LEX LOCI (The Law Of This Place), I, Hector, appoint you as my Second In Command."

That was it. Sledger was now officially Second in Command and, as Hector placed a strip on his shoulder so all would know of his new appointment, Sledger puffed his chest out with pride. With a large yawn Hector nestled down in his chair. He was obviously getting ready for a sleep and he dismissed Sledger and Janous.

Janous was so proud and as the two of them walked wing in wing back to the hospital a true sense of happiness reigned over them. Out in the courtyard they saw Sweeney and Todd sitting with Ripper on one of the roofs. Sledger told Janous to ignore them, as Hector would deal with Ripper later. Janous entered the hospital a very happy raven.

Fred and Charlie, unaware of all the events at the Tower, were still waiting patiently for The Great Gob. The two brothers wondered if he was ever going to show. Just then a strange wind began to blow.

"He is coming," shouted Belvedere at the top of his voice, and then, as if by magic, hundreds of Gronkiedoddles appeared from nowhere. Stronger the wind blew and out over the Thames a blue sphere appeared.

Fred and Charlie were so excited that at last they were going to meet the Ruler of all the animals in London. Larger and larger the sphere grew until it burst into a thousand sparks and before them stood The Great Gob.

3

chapter

The challenge of the quest is set

Fred and Charlie could not believe their eyes. Before them stood The Great Gob dressed in fine blue robes and he towered above everyone. The cheering was deafening. Fred and Charlie were so proud to be part of such a gathering. The River Thames was as still as a mirror and the atmosphere seemed electric. Suddenly, with a loud clap of his hands, all the Gronkiedoddles fell silent and the deep voice of The Great Gob was heard.

"We are gathered here tonight to witness a very special occasion. For many months now I have been watching all the animals and the Gronkiedoddles here in London. I have been searching for qualities that might be those of a leader. The raven known as Honourous, The Grand Master of all the animals, is about to retire and a replacement for his position has to be found. I have considered Plodger, the chief of all the pigeons, but he tends to gossip too much. I have considered Hector, the chief of all the ravens, but he is too old. We need fresh young blood that will carry on the tradition of being Grand Master for many years to come. Until earlier I had given up hope on finding anyone, but then Belvedere returned home after a very difficult journey from helping the homeless, and explained how the two ravens had helped him in a time of desperate need. So impressed was I with this act of compassion and desire to help a fellow animal and Gronk that I felt the need to call this meeting."

Another cheer rang out amongst the Gronkiedoddle's and Belvedere took a bow, but Fred and Charlie were quite confused about all the commotion. After a short while The Great Gob once again raised his large arms and silence fell.

"Having now seen Fred and Charlie and knowing their father from old, I have decided to set the quest for The Great London Adventure. If Belvedere, Fred and Charlie should accept this quest and successfully complete the challenge, they will become joint Grand Masters of the Whole of London. On this quest you will meet many good animals, but there are some bad ones, so be careful. The clues that you will solve will lead you to your next destination until finally you will finish at the Tower of London. There we shall present to you the book of The Great London Adventure that contains many secrets. You will then be crowned Grand Masters."

All Fred, Charlie and Belvedere could do was to thank The Great Gob as a huge cheer rang out. Many Gronkiedoddles were patting Fred and Charlie on the back and hugging Belvedere. Hats and scarves were thrown into the air and whistles of joy echoed across the Thames. The Great Gob shook Fred and Charlie by the wing and wished them well. Turning to Belvedere, he laid out his hand and the tiny Gronk stepped onto his palm. The Great Gob rose Belvedere high, level with his face and kissed him on his head.

"Good luck, Belvedere and make all the Gronkiedoddles proud." With that The Great Gob placed Belvedere safely back on the ground. Addressing the crowd once again and gaining order, The Great Gob stood tall.

" Remember, my three adventurers, take care, use the wise ones you will meet, and stay clear of the evil ones that will hinder you. Animals like Mustafat, Lucif, Saber, Foil and even Ripper at the Tower, may cause you harm. Avoid these few and you will succeed in your quest." The Great Gob then pulled out an envelope from inside his robes. "In this envelope you will find the address of Tibbs, the sparrow from the Animal Tourist Board. She will have your first clue and a map that will help you find your way. Now, I must go and you must report back to the Tower where the ravens will help you prepare for the quest. I will send word to Hector."

As the winds began to blow once again The Great Gob stood back by the water's edge and with yet another burst of sparks he left as he had arrived. Suddenly Fred, Charlie and Belvedere felt all alone as behind them all the Gronkiedoddles had disappeared. On the ground in front of them Belvedere noticed that something was shining where the Great Gob had been standing. Picking it up, the little Gronk noticed that it was a very old compass and on the back was an inscription.

FOR TRAVELLERS TO FIND THEIR WAY
SO THEY MAY SEE ANOTHER DAY

read Belvedere out loud. He was so pleased that he had found the compass he held it close to his chest. Fred and Charlie, however, were still in shock after their visit from The Great Gob. Fred broke the silence amongst the three of them.

"Well then, I think we need to get back to the Tower and see Hector. We can open this envelope in the dry and plan for our journey."

Belvedere and Charlie agreed. They were all tired and wet and needed some food. It was still too early for Fred, Charlie and Belvedere to believe what was happening to them and the challenge they were about to embark on. A journey of this size was going to be very exhausting and many plans had to be made. The sun had started to rise and the sound of the city traffic could be heard.

"Okay, chaps, let's go and see Hector, wagons roll," said Charlie in a voice of a famous cowboy film star, followed by a very large yawn.

Fred whispered in Belvedere's ear and explained that Charlie was trying to act like John Wayne, the big American movie star, but all Belvedere could do was roll his eyes. He had got used to Charlie's little ways and found them funny.

Time was getting short and the three of them had to set off. The Tower would soon be full of Rucksacks (Tourists) and it would be impossible to get into the Tower undetected.

Belvedere led the way from the meeting place and once again onto the cobbles of the street that led to the Tower. Finding their way back was not that difficult at all, as Belvedere was an excellent guide. En route home Fred, Charlie and Belvedere bumped straight into Plodger, the Chief of all the Pigeons. With a tilt of his hat he said a polite 'hello' and scurried off. But being so nosey, Plodger flew up onto one of the roofs near by to watch Fred and Charlie. He had not seen Belvedere at all, until, that is, he saw the Gronk run ahead to see if the coast was clear for Fred and Charlie to enter the Tower through the main gates. Two ravens out at this time in the morning and a Gronk so near by. Plodger knew that something was going on and he had to find out what!

As the bright early morning sun cascaded through the trees at the Tower Fred, Charlie and Belvedere, who was now hidden in Charlie's feathers, made their way through the grounds to find Hector's office. Suddenly there was something shining from one of the roofs and Fred and Charlie noticed Ripper hiding behind one of the turrets. Not wanting to get caught by Ripper, Fred and Charlie hurried along.

The Tower seemed different this morning. Everything was quiet and, apart from Ripper, there was not a raven in sight. Once out of the grounds of the Tower and into the many corridors that were beneath the Tower Fred and Charlie were amazed at how quickly they found Hector's office. Belvedere kept out of sight just in case they bumped into Ripper, who might have followed them.

Hector's office door was now in front of them and they could hear the snores of the old raven coming from inside. Belvedere got down on his hands and knees and looked through a crack in the door. Hector was sitting with his feet up on his desk and had his wings behind his head. One of his feathers had fallen out and with each breath he took it rose and fell.

"He is sound asleep, I think we will need a hammer to wake him up," said Belvedere dusting himself down. Together Fred and Charlie banged on the door with all their might. Inside the office they could hear the stirring of Hector. Then the snoring stopped and turned to a muttering, but still Hector neither opened the door nor summoned them to enter. So Fred and Charlie knocked even harder this time and Hector's muffled voice rang out 'Enter'.

Belvedere hid behind Charlie as they entered the office. Hector who was still half asleep opened his eyes and turned to look at Fred and Charlie. Suddenly Hector's eyes were open wide and he lost his balance and fell off his chair. As he appeared beak first from under his desk Hector, although embarrassed, seemed very pleased to see them and as he got to his feet he dusted himself down.

"Don't be fooled by that, all part of the training, can't be too careful nowadays. Impressive though, I was under that desk before you could blink. Now, how are you, where have you been? We have all been so worried. Sit down you must be exhausted."

Hector offered Fred and Charlie two chairs and slightly confused about Hector's concern, they sat down and explained the whole story from beginning to end. Hector listened with great interest and nodded from time to time, followed by a grunt or a 'carry on'. Belvedere who had become quite bored of being ignored decided to take a closer look at the Chief of all the ravens.

Very slowly and very quietly Belvedere climbed up onto Hector's desk. Hector, who was still listening, but with his eyes shut, had no idea that now he was being observed by Belvedere, the Gronkiedoddle, until that is he opened his eyes.

Hector let out a loud cry, as did Belvedere. Hector instinctively swept his wing across the desk and sent Belvedere flying to the floor. Hector jumped to his feet.

"I mean to say, what was that, it, him, her, er..., oh hang on that was a Gronkiedoddle, er..... Belvedere I presume."

Belvedere had climbed back up onto the desk by this time and was standing with his hands on his hips with a stern look on his face. Hector apologised to the little Gronk and Fred explained all about how he was the Gronkiedoddle that they had given a lift to and how The Great Gob had wanted to meet the three of them together, which is why they had left their guarding duties earlier. Hector held out a wing to Belvedere.

"Pleased to meet you, little fellow."

Belvedere returned the greeting and shook Hector's wing. Just then, however, there was a knock at the door. Belvedere hid behind a large stack of files and Hector shouted 'Enter'. Through the large oak door walked a stranger to the Tower.

"Message for Hector, Chief of the pigeons, no, sorry ravens."

Hector acknowledged who he was and the messenger left having given Hector an official-looking envelope. Belvedere immediately noticed the seal. It was from The Great Gob. Hector opened the letter and read it to himself muttering as always. Folding the envelope he placed it in his desk drawer.

"Grand Masters, eh, all three of you. Well, what an honour. Your father will be very proud of you. But this quest is not easy you know. Oh no, I have heard that some have undertaken the challenge and never been seen again. But never mind, we have much work to do," said Hector who seemed to be a bit flustered. Fred thought it was because he had been turned down for the job of Grand Master, but he was not going to ask. Time passed by as the four of them chatted and made plans for the journey. Fred and Charlie had no idea how much was involved in planning. Belvedere, who travelled a great deal helping the homeless at night, was very expert and the two brothers were glad he was coming along.

The map and the address of Tibbs from the Animal Tourist Board were laid out on the desk. Hector did not know where the address was located, but he knew a raven that did. Just then there was another knock at the door. Belvedere once again hid behind the pile of files and once again Hector's voice of authority boomed 'Enter'.

As the door opened Fred and Charlie could not believe their eyes. Their father had arrived. He looked very tired and his feathers looked very ruffled. He obviously had been flying all night. Fred and Charlie's father ran over to his sons and gave them a huge hug.

"You are safe. Sybulus would not tell me anything, but I knew it had to be about you two. Now, what have you been up to? Come out with it, tell me the truth."

Sybulus pushed his way forward as Bostrum checked his sons for cuts and bruises, convinced they had been in some sort of trouble.

"All present and correct, sir."

"Thank you, Sybulus, you have done a good job, but now I want you to work out a route to the Animal Tourist Board at Victoria train station. I shall explain later, but this must been done very quickly."

Sybulus saluted without question and left the room to plan the route. It was then that Hector noticed an old raven that was seated at the back of his office. To Hector's surprise it was Honourous.

"Honourous, what are you doing here?" questioned Hector. This was the great Honourous whom The Great Gob had spoken about, thought Fred and Charlie. Honourous explained how Bostrum, Fred and Charlie's father, had been called back to the Tower and he knew that meant something serious was going on. So he had taken it upon himself to follow and see if he could help. He had also heard a rumour that The Great Gob might be setting the quest of The Great London Adventure to some ravens and a Gronkiedoddle. Hector looked at Bostrum who could not contain himself any longer.

"Okay, what is going on here? Honourous insisted on coming and now the mention of The Great Gob. Come on, Hector, what is it?"

Hector explained the story of how his sons had helped Belvedere, the Gronkiedoddle, and how The Great Gob had sent a messenger explaining that Fred, Charlie and Belvedere had been set the quest. Should they succeed they would become Grand Masters. Just then Belvedere stepped out from behind the pile of files. Bostrum could not believe his eyes or ears. Honourous, who was used to Gronks, walked over and patted Belvedere on the head with his wing.

"Nice to see you again, sir," said Belvedere, very proud to be in the company of Honourous. Hector sent word for some food so they all could eat and build their strength. Bostrum was very proud of his sons and sat talking to them whilst Hector, Honourous and Belvedere made a list for the preparations for their journey. In no time at all a raven had delivered a tray of goodies of bread, milk and raw pastry from the kitchens. Everyone ate until their stomachs were nearly bursting and now tiredness was taking over and Fred and Charlie were nearly asleep. Honourous suggested that he and Bostrum took the two brothers and Belvedere to the dormitory where they could get some sleep as it was going to be a long day and night for the three travellers.

Before they left Fred and Charlie asked if Sledger was all right and Hector, who did not want to worry them, explained that he was fine.

Belvedere decided it would be better if he stayed with Hector and helped with the plans, Gronks needed very little sleep and he did not feel that tired. Belvedere sat down on a roll of sellotape and studied the map with Hector as Fred and Charlie left with their father and Honourous.

Sweeney and Todd had left Ripper on one of the roofs. They needed to sleep. Whilst Ripper watched the Rucksacks below he planned how he could get even with Sledger and capture the Gronkiedoddle, should he ever appear. He also wondered what Fred and Charlie were up to.

Back in Hector's office Belvedere had finally fallen asleep behind the pile of files and Hector had covered him up with a handkerchief. Even the knock at the door had not disturbed Belvedere. Sledger entered the office limping and with his head hung low. Hector asked him what the matter was, concerned that Ripper may have tried to bully him again, but Sledger explained that Ripper had not been seen. He then went on to explain his problem.

"It's the pigeons, sir. There is a rumour going around that Fred and Charlie are going to take over the animal kingdom. Plodger started the rumour and now all the pigeons are landing on the lawns. It is making our job very difficult. I mean to say, what can we do in front of all the Rucksacks."

Hector paced up and down his office rubbing his beak in thought before finally turning to Sledger. "Sledger you are Second In Command now and this is what I want you to do. I want you to go to Plodger. You will find him at the Tower front gates. I want you to tell him to stop these rumours right now, or I shall walk the lawns and he knows what that will mean, Trouble with a capital T. If these rumours do not stop, then I shall ban him and all his pigeons from the Tower and the surrounding mile. No more crumbs for them..."

Before Sledger could respond, Belvedere let out a huge sneeze and appeared from behind his pile of files. Sledger's beak fell open and Hector was certain that Sledger's eyes grew ten times their normal size. Hector rushed over and offered Sledger a wing of support as he was convinced Sledger was going to faint.

Hector explained that Fred and Charlie had returned safely and all about their forthcoming journey for the quest of The Great London Adventure. He also explained that Belvedere, who now was sitting back on his roll of sellotape, had been the one who had led Fred and Charlie away from their duties the night before to meet with The Great Gob.

Sledger did not know whether to shake Belvedere by the hand or snarl his beak at him. After all it was this Gronk that had left all the gold dust behind that had caused him to go to Ripper and have all his feathers pulled out. Sledger did not have time to react for Belvedere had burst out laughing as he had just spotted Sledger's legs. Belvedere, realising now how insensitive he had been, apologised and Sledger left to carry out his orders and deal with the rumours.

Once at the front gates Sledger bounded up to Plodger with his chest all puffed out.

"You see ravens taking over, told you. Why else would a raven come outside the Tower to where we are?" jeered Plodger to the other pigeons. Turning round, Plodger pointed at a wall. "Look, they are taking over and have a new leader, Lucif."

Sledger had not got a clue what Plodger was talking about. Then it dawned on him.

"You stupid pigeon, Lucif is not a raven, he is a cat and he is the meanest cat of all time, stalking London day and night. Now listen, you gossip, I have a message for you from Hector."

Plodger, feeling rather silly about the mix up over Lucif, stood and listened as Sledger told him exactly what Hector had said, but in a more forceful tone. Concern washed over Plodger's face. He could not afford to lose his place at the Tower gates and neither could any of the other pigeons. They all had children to feed. He agreed to stop spreading rumours about the ravens, but was very concerned about the writing on the wall. Sledger walked over to take a closer look. The writing read...

Banish The Pigeons today - Keep Britain Tidy
LUCIF

Lucif had obviously been at the Tower the night before. But still Sledger thought the note sounded a little soft for Lucif. They would all have to keep their eyes open. Sledger assured Plodger that he would report the writing to Hector straight away. In the meantime Plodger was to keep his beak shut.

All the pigeons muttered and gathered around Plodger as Sledger walked back through the Tower's main gates. It was then that Sledger noticed Ripper laughing on top of one of the roofs. Maybe it was Ripper that had written the message on the wall thought Sledger as he walked past him, resisting the temptation to look up.

Hector, unaware of all the commotion outside, had gathered some things together and placed them in a very old leather satchel. Hector had sent word over the raven internet between his office and central raven control somewhere deep inside the Tower for further preparation and to gather certain ravens in the dining room. The raven internet was actually two coke cans tied together on a piece of string, but it worked quite well, although you had to talk instead of typing.

It was now time for them to wake Fred and Charlie and set up a control centre in the dining room. Belvedere climbed inside the satchel and, as Hector had placed it on his shoulder, he got into a comfortable position for the walk to the dormitory and the dining room.

Once inside the sleeping quarters, Hector noticed that Bostrum was already up and about, Honourous was just waking, and Fred and Charlie were sound asleep. Hector rang a bell that hung on the wall and the two brothers began to open their eyes. Bostrum laughed at his two sons as they rustled about making funny grunting noises. Sometimes he had even had to throw water over them to get them up in the mornings back at the nest, but today he thought better of it.

Fred and Charlie swung their legs out over the side of the bed, rubbing their eyes. Bostrum told them to go and wash their beaks whilst Hector, Honourous and he had a chat. Belvedere in the meantime had climbed out of the satchel and sat down on a big fluffy pillow.

"What's the matter, Hector?" questioned Honourous as the old chief paced up and down.

"We have a problem with the pigeons. They are getting restless and think that a raven is going to take over the animal kingdom. I have sent Sledger to go and sort it out, but

I don't like it. This sort of thing causes unrest amongst the ravens. We have to get Fred, Charlie and Belvedere off on this quest as soon as possible."

Bostrum and Honourous agreed. Hector also explained that he had organised the dining room to be turned into a central room for co-ordination so they could plan the journey properly. Without a word Honourous was on his way to the dining room. Just as Honourous left the room Fred and Charlie returned with their beaks polished and their feathers dusted. They looked so much better after a few hours sleep. Everyone had gathered in the dining room. Hector wiped a huge blackboard clean and was making detailed lists of everything the three adventurers were going to need. Bostrum studied a map of London with great interest. Honourous was showing Fred, Charlie and Belvedere a book that contained photographs of all the bad animals they might encounter including one of Lucif, the brains behind the great cat food robbery many years before. Belvedere, who was sitting on a pepper pot, suddenly ran off to hide as Bascer entered the room.

"Ah, Bascer, good you got the message then. I want you to make a fine leather satchel for Fred and Charlie. They are going on a long and dangerous journey, so make it of the finest leather." Bascer threw his wings in the air and shook his head in disbelief.

"A satchel. I ask you. I knew these two would be a problem. Now they want a satchel, and made of leather. It will cost so much money and Bessie will be not very pleased. She hoped to bake this afternoon."

Hector ignored the complaints from Bascer and ordered him to get on with it as soon as possible. He hated it when Bascer moaned so much. As Bascer left the room, Fred and Charlie said 'hello' but Bascer was too busy to consider saying 'hello'. He was too deep in thought.

Word had soon spread that Fred and Charlie were home safe and that they were going on a journey of extreme importance and, as the dining room got busier and busier, presents began to arrive wishing them well. But the best present arrived when Fray and Bentos, the Tower's raven's chefs, arrived with food parcels for the journey. Hector thanked them for the parcels and noticed that they seemed to be hanging about.

"That's all, chefs, thank you," said Hector in his stern voice. The chef's left the room still looking around, they were obviously looking for Belvedere. Then, to Fred and Charlie's delight, Sledger entered the dining room. On seeing the two brothers Sledger limped over as fast as he could to greet them.

"Cor deary me, I thought we would never see you two again. How are you? Seen my legs? Ripper's doing all that. Still, all's well that ends well. I have been made Second In Command and Janous and I are to be married." Sledger spoke so fast it was hard for Fred and Charlie to keep up and understand what he was saying. Hector let Sledger chat away for a while, but was very keen to learn what Plodger had said, so he decided it was time to interrupt the reunion.

"Can I have a word, Sledger?"

Hector and Sledger huddled in a corner as he explained what Plodger had said and about the writing on the wall. Hector seemed quite concerned and flustered as he always did when he was thinking. With a snap of his wing tip Hector ordered Sledger to bring Ripper to the dining room and at the same time to get Janous to make up a first aid kit for Fred and Charlie. Sledger left straight away, but not before giving the two brothers a quick wave good bye.

The table in front of Fred and Charlie had become filled with everything they were going to need and Charlie was concerned about how they were going to carry it all. One thing was certain was that Belvedere was too small to carry anything they were going to need. Well, maybe he could manage the map, thought Fred!

Suddenly the dining room fell silent. Ripper had entered. Before Hector had a chance to do anything Honourous stepped forward.

"I want a word with you," said Honourous, dragging Ripper into a corner so no one could hear. Ripper stood to attention in front of the old wise bird as Honourous whispered into his ear in a menacing way.

"Now, listen to me, Ripper. If I hear that you have disrupted this journey in any way I shall take you to the tar dump myself and make sure that you never, never leave. Do I make myself clear?" Ripper nodded and walked back to Hector with his head hung low.

"Ripper reporting for duty, sir."

Hector was very impressed with Ripper's true guard's posture and ordered him to guard his office door and not to move. Ripper saluted and marched from the room. As Ripper left, Bascer returned with the most beautiful leather satchel. Hector placed a wing on his shoulder and patted him on the back as everyone gathered to see his craftsmanship.

"You have excelled yourself, Bascer. This work is truly great. I shall make sure you get an award for this."

Bascer beamed with pride, but then suddenly caught sight of Belvedere. As quick as a flash Bascer had his tape measure out and was measuring the Gronk. Then without a word he rushed from the room. As everyone looked about in surprise at Bascer's actions, Hector began sniffing the air. A strange scent had floated into the room. It was the scent of Piccadilly Number 5, the very best perfume a raveness could wear. Turning round Hector, Honourous and Bostrum noticed that Janous was standing in the doorway to the dining hall. Janous glided across the room to where everyone was standing and placed a small box on the table.

"The First Aid kit you asked for, sir."

Even Belvedere's mouth dropped open at the beauty of the
raven that stood before them. Much to his delight she blew
him a kiss. Fred and Charlie, however, were even happier as
she kissed them on their beaks. Hector had never noticed the
true beauty of Janous as she once again spoke in her soft
velvet voice. "Sir, do you mind if I sing these three
adventurers a song before they leave?"

"Not at all," replied Hector. So, with a flutter of her long
eyelashes, Janous began to sing, Sledger, who was standing
by the door, could not believe his ears. As Janous leant back
with her wings outstretched her voice filled the room, and
what a beautiful voice it was. The entire group of ravens
looked at Sledger in jealousy. He was a very lucky raven to be
marrying Janous. Fray and Bentos had even come from their
kitchens to see who was singing. At the window a few pigeons
had landed, but Hector closed the curtains. This was a
private show.

Bostrum turned on a torch and followed Janous around with
the beam, just as if she were on at the London Palladium
Theatre. As the song came to an end Janous made her way to
the door and on the last note she disappeared from sight and
was gone. The room erupted in applause. Janous was a star.
Sledger pushed his chest out in pride and took a bow on
her behalf.

Just after Janous had left and the applause had died down

Bascer once again came rushing into the room searching for Belvedere. Hector escorted Bascer over to the Gronk and the raven tailor placed a tiny flying jacket in front of Belvedere.

"My wife and I have made this for you. We know that Fred and Charlie's landings are not very good, so this might give you some protection. It will also keep the cold out when flying at night."

Belvedere thanked Bascer from the bottom of his heart and immediately tried his new jacket on which fitted perfectly. The preparations were complete and, as Hector clapped his wings, all the ravens formed a line, Belvedere climbed into the satchel and Charlie placed it around his neck. They were ready to begin their adventure.

Hector began the march and everyone followed in step. Through the corridors they marched and Bostrum began to sing an old army marching song. Soon everyone was joining in including Fred and Charlie.

"Here we go and off we set, hoping never to see a vet."

As they marched and sang, more ravens joined the procession until nearly all the ravens were in the march. Hector brought the procession to a halt at his office door where Ripper was keeping guard. Pushing Ripper to one side Hector entered his office and shut the door. In no time at all, he was back out dressed in his finest robes of the Royal Raven Order, only worn on very special occasions.

Hector raised his wings and once again the marching and singing started. Ripper seized the chance of getting into Hector's good books and gathered together the long train of robe that trailed behind Hector and carried it for him.

Outside Fred and Charlie noticed that many animals had gathered on the lawns of the Tower and the roof was full to bursting point. Fred and Charlie felt like film stars and Belvedere tried to see as much as he could from his satchel. Hector's speech was brief, wishing them a safe journey and success in their plight for the quest.

With a hug from their father Fred and Charlie were ready for take off. Charlie made a few last minute adjustments to the satchel and they were ready. Fred turned to his brother as everyone watched.

"Okay, Foxtrot Leader to Alpha November Ready For Take Off." Charlie smiled at his brother.

"Okay roger that. This Is Flight BA147009 ready for take off, destination London, we hope you have an enjoyable flight, we will be flying at three thousand feet if the weather is clear."

Charlie hoped that Belvedere could hear. After all, it was very important that his passenger was treated correctly. With a quick nod to their friends and a tip of their wing to Hector, Honourous and their father, Fred and Charlie began their take off. Charlie was having difficulty in gaining speed with the weight of the satchel and it looked at one point as if he would not get airborne, but just in time he began to rise into the air.

Sweeney and Todd, who were watching everything from the rooftops, suddenly became worried as Charlie flew over them. All that was heard was the sound of a dull thud and cry. Looking back Charlie noticed that the satchel had knocked Sweeney clean off the roof much to the delight of everyone gathered below.

High in the skies Fred and Charlie could see the whole of London. Their adventure had truly began.

4
chapter
Two stops en route

With their route planned in great detail by Sybulus, Fred and Charlie flew up the Thames towards the many bridges they knew that they were going to have to navigate before turning right towards Victoria train station.

In some strange way the two brothers felt relieved that they were now on their own with Belvedere as their travelling companion. In the distance the rays of sunshine sparkled as they bounced off the many satellite dishes on Telecom Tower. It had been a long time since Fred and Charlie had seen their home and they hoped that the nest was safe and sound.

Before long Fred was beginning to look uncertain and Charlie asked him if anything was wrong. Looking about the vast skyline below, Fred explained that all the buildings looked the same and he hoped that they were going in the right direction. Charlie tried to reassure his brother, but the problem now was that Fred had put doubt into Charlie's mind. Not wanting to risk getting lost Fred and Charlie decided to land and refer to their map, with Belvedere's help of course. Fred looked for a suitable spot to land and suddenly spied the perfect place.

"Down there, Charlie. Perfect place, we'll land there," shouted Fred. Down the two brothers swooped forgetting that Belvedere would be crumpled in one corner of the satchel with such a steep descent. As Fred and Charlie came into land, they discovered that the gap between the tables and chairs that lined their runway was too narrow and, not being experienced landing experts, disaster was bound to happen. The landing spot that Fred had chosen was a large ship that was now used as a restaurant, and the other problem they were soon to face was that the decks of the ship were very slippery.

With no grip from their claws, Fred and Charlie sent chairs flying in all directions before they finally came to a halt with a bump against a large oak door. Had it been open this would have meant that Fred and Charlie would had fallen into the engine room, deep below the ship's decks.

Belvedere staggered from the satchel that had spun across the deck as Charlie had lost control. He tried very hard to keep on his feet, but with all the spinning he had totally lost his sense of balance and he sat down hard with a bump. Gathering his senses, Belvedere looked up at Fred and Charlie.

"You stupid idiot birds, you could have killed me," shouted Belvedere at the top of his voice, still shaking from his experience.

"We are really sorry, Belvedere. It won't happen again. It is just that the tables and chairs got in the way and the decks were like an ice rink," explained Fred and Charlie together. They were genuinely sorry and concerned that they might have hurt the little chap, but Belvedere simply grunted and muttered under his breath about the lawns at the Tower of London and now the decks of a ship. Silence fell as the three adventurers looked around and saw the debris they had caused. Tables and chairs were upside down and scattered all over the place.

Not saying a word Belvedere got to his feet and rubbed his bruises whilst Fred and Charlie explained that they had landed to make sure they were going in the right direction. Belvedere, who this time was shaking his head, disappeared inside the satchel and returned carrying the map.

With the map spread out in front of them, Belvedere used his fine compass which he kept in his inside pocket and began working out the co-ordinates to Victoria train station. Fred and Charlie watched as Belvedere looked this way and that and with a tiny ruler marked the map very carefully. Just then, as Fred let out a large yawn, something blew into his mouth. Coughing and spluttering, Fred immediately spat it out, only to discover that he had nearly swallowed a book of matches, which is very dangerous. On the front cover of the matches there was some writing and Fred read aloud.

"The Tattershall Castle, fine wines, good food and a top class night club. Wow, we have landed on a floating Rucksacks, fun emporium." Charlie's eyes opened wide, and Belvedere looked up with a grin on his face.

"Mine is a soda, if you are buying?" exclaimed Charlie. Fred and Charlie's favourite drink was soda. The very mention of it sent shivers down the two brothers' spines with delight. Belvedere was quite fond of soda as well, but they had more important things to do than sit around all day drinking their favourite drink.

Belvedere returned to reading the map whilst Fred and Charlie dreamed of sitting on the deck for the rest of the day, but the peace and quiet of where they were sitting was disturbed as they heard voices.

Belvedere quickly gathered the map up and climbed into the satchel. Just as he closed the satchel flap two Rucksacks (tourists) came round the corner. Fred nudged Charlie in the ribs and told him to act as normal as he could.

"Ahh, look, Harry, two birds having a rest. And look at their fine clothes. They must be from a circus and they must be lost," said the woman who bent down to take a closer look. Charlie curled his beak up to look as menacing as he possibly could. He had heard how humans sometimes captured birds and took them home, instead of calling people that can help.

"Don't be silly, dear, they are ravens from the Tower of London. Probably on a day off and doing a bit of sightseeing just like us. Now leave them alone, before they peck you," said the woman's husband. Charlie still kept his beak curled up until the woman had sat down. With no time to lose Fred and Charlie had to leave the ship as soon as possible.

"Hold on tight, Belvedere," whispered Charlie as he and his brother got to their feet. Belvedere whispered directions from the safety of his satchel and prepared for another take off.

In no time at all Fred and Charlie were airborne without any crashes on the way. Looking back they noticed the two Rucksacks sitting and laughing at Charlie because he was carrying a satchel. They were saying that he looked like a stork. This was too much for Fred. No one called his brother a stork.

With the look of a World War Two bomber Fred dived down to where the Rucksacks were sitting and swooped past them grabbing some bread, before soaring back up into the sky to join his brother. The two Rucksacks sat in amazement, not knowing what to say or do. Charlie, however, was not very pleased with his brother.

"Fred, you should not have done that. What would our father say? He told us many times that it was wrong to steal and here you are swooping down and stealing bread. You will get us sent to Ping Ping, the famous jail, if you are not careful."

Fred was astounded at his brother's outburst and deep down he knew he was right. It was wrong to steal. Fred promised Charlie he would never steal again, as the two of them flew side by side up the Thames once again rejoining their journey.

Over the Houses of Parliament they flew. Belvedere was quite happy and comfortable in his satchel and the flight was very relaxing, so much so that he was sucking on one of his cinnamon sticks. But little did Belvedere know that the sight of Big Ben and the lawns of Parliament would be too much of a temptation for Fred and Charlie. As Belvedere began to feel the descent, panic overwhelmed him. Another landing was about to happen and he braced himself for the inevitable bumps.

The touchdown on the grass was perfect, not a claw mark or even a skid. Pleased with themselves, Fred and Charlie puffed out their chests and walked round for a while. Then all of a sudden they heard someone was clapping. Turning round, they noticed a very well dressed mole leaning up against the walls of Parliament. Belvedere popped his head out of the satchel to see what was going on and ducked out of sight when he saw the mole. They had not landed at the Tourist Board, thought Belvedere. What were Fred and Charlie doing now? All Belvedere could hear was muffled voices.

"'Morning. Moody Morgan, the mole of the Houses of Parliament," said the mole, in a very well spoken accent.

"You have to have permission to land here, you know, and I don't see any landing passes." Moody Morgan continued to talk non-stop for at least fifteen minutes, not giving the two brothers chance to say a word. Fred and Charlie were amazed. Even Belvedere had come out of his satchel to see what was going on and had sat down on the grass with his head in his hands wishing Moody would stop talking. Then, without warning, Moody dashed off saying that he hoped he would meet them again soon and that it had been great talking to them. Fred and Charlie looked at each other in disbelief. They had not said a word to him.

"When you have quite finished, do you think we might be able to get on our way now?" said Belvedere a little annoyed that Fred and Charlie had wasted so much time. Fred and Charlie agreed and were soon back in the air. As he banked round to follow his brother's lead, Fred hoped that it would not be a long time before they revisited the Houses of Parliament.

Charlie was finding flying very hard going with the added weight of the satchel and with a cross-wind that had now developed. Sweat fell from his beak as he flew. With each flap of their wings Fred and Charlie knew they were getting closer to the Animal Tourist Information Centre. Below them cars stopped and started and people went about their business, unaware that above them history was being made as the three adventurers flew closer to finding out their first clue. Then suddenly Fred shouted across to Charlie.

"Look over there, that huge blue sign on the roof. The Tourist Information Centre. That has to be it, Charlie, come on." Fred banked round and headed for the sign with Charlie trying to keep up. Belvedere was relieved that soon he would be able to stretch his legs. "One, Two, Three, Touchdown," counted Fred as he and his brother landed safely on the roof. Taking off the satchel Charlie joined his brother as he peered over the edge of the rooftop. Below many Rucksacks (tourists) rushed about. A loudspeaker rang out from the train station next door and added to the atmosphere of the place. Fred and Charlie had never seen so many people at one time. With the coast clear, Charlie helped Belvedere from his satchel and, as he rubbed his legs, Charlie had a huge stretch.

All they had to do now was to find Tibbs and get on with the quest that they had been set. But how were they going to find Tibbs, thought Charlie, as he looked about. Then, without warning, Fred whispered to Charlie.

"Charlie, look at this."

Charlie once again made his way to the edge of the roof as Fred pointed to the corner of the street below. They were being watched.

"Look, Charlie, that cat has been watching us since we landed. I think that is one of the cats that Honourous showed us in the photograph albums back at the Tower. He is one of the cats we have to be careful of, I am sure."

With a lick of his lips the cat stared at the two brothers. Fred felt very uneasy, as the cat seemed to lick his lips in a mean but purposeful way. Charlie, who was equally unsure, tried to comfort his brother.

"Don't worry, I will save us if he decides to attack. They don't call me Bambo for nothing, you know."

Fred just looked at his brother. As if he could do anything if the cat decided to attack them! Fred suggested that they move away from the edge of the roof and try and find Tibbs as quickly as possible. Belvedere explained that the cat might have a hard job climbing up so high, but thought it was a good idea that they found Tibbs. Just then, high in the sky, a flock of birds were saying good bye to a very well dressed sparrow, who with a last wave of her wing began to fly down to Fred and Charlie. Daintily Tibbs landed next to Fred, Charlie and Belvedere.

"Hello, my name is Tibbs. I have been expecting you. Oh, this is so exciting. You on the quest, and me to give you your first clue." Tibbs shook Fred and Charlie by their wings and leant over to shake Belvedere's hand.

"Come on, follow me," said Tibbs, as she delicately walked along the canopy to a tiny little door, removing a key from her jacket. Tibbs opened the door.

"Here we are, all safe and sound," said Tibbs as Fred, Charlie and Belvedere joined her in what looked like her office. Fred and Charlie thought that they would not mention the cat outside, for fear of seeming cowards. Belvedere sat on Tibbs' desk watching her very carefully. As she turned round she smiled at him and the little Gronk blushed.

On the office walls were many maps of London and

photographs of far away places. Fred found them quite fascinating, but his attention was soon drawn back to Tibbs as she began to speak once again.

"Now, as you know, the Great Gob has asked me to give you your first clue. You have a lot to learn whilst on your quest about the many animals that live here in London. Once you have solved all the clues you are to report back to the Tower of London where The Great Gob will meet you. Do you understand?" Fred, Charlie and Belvedere nodded in agreement that they understood. So Tibbs continued. "I can not help you with your first clue. You have to solve it for yourselves."

Once again the three travellers nodded in agreement. Tibbs then opened a drawer and removed a gold envelope with a red seal on the back. Handing the envelope to Charlie, she wished them luck and told them to open it.

Charlie could hardly wait and, as the others looked on, he tore open the envelope. Inside there was a gold card with writing on it. Charlie pulled the card out and handed it to Fred who read it aloud.

MARYLEBONE ROAD HOLDS THE SECRET
A DOME YOU WILL SEE
INDICATED ON THE BACK OF THIS LEAFLET

Fred and Charlie looked at each other in total confusion. What did the clue mean? Belvedere turned the card over and on the back was a map, but nothing that indicated a dome. All three of them looked at Tibbs for some help.

"Okay, look, I will help you on this clue, but you must promise never to tell The Great Gob." Everyone agreed and handed the clue to Tibbs. With a smile on her beak she walked over to a photograph that hung on the office wall.

"The dome in the clue is Madame Tussaud's, on Marylebone Road. It is not far from here and there you will find hundreds of wax models. The dome, by the way, is sixty-seven feet high, so I don't think you will miss it. It is inside Madame Tussaud's that you will find your next clue."

Charlie picked the clue up from the desk and as he turned it over to look at the map again as if by magic the map had disappeared and another clue had replaced it. Carefully Charlie read aloud.

IN THE TRUE SPIRIT OF LONDON
YOU WILL FIND YOUR FIRST CLUE
ATTACHED TO A PIGEON
DRESSED IN RED, WHITE AND BLUE

Fred, Charlie and Belvedere were none the wiser, but Tibbs did not utter a word. Suddenly Charlie shouted out aloud.

"Well really, you would have to be Shylock Bungalow to work this out." Everyone burst into laughter. What Charlie meant to say was Sherlock Holmes, the great London Detective.

Tibbs and the three adventurers chatted away for some time and as the four-thirty train rattled to a stop at platform three below Fred, Charlie and Belvedere knew the time had come for them to leave. Tibbs had helped them as much as she dared and had told them to look out for the caretaker at Madame Tussaud's, Doc Curtious, as he was certain to help them further.

Once out on the roof again Charlie cut a small hole in the satchel so Belvedere could see where they were going and help with the map reading. Fred had packed some of the food parcels into his pockets to try and lighten Charlie's load and as they were about to set off Tibbs looked about and told them to gather closer. Quietly she whispered, "That cat you saw earlier, that was Mustafat. Stay out of his way and you will be safe."

With that Tibbs turned round and rushed back into her office, not looking back once. Fred and Charlie gulped at the thought of Mustafat, as he was a very large cat. Fred had been right, he had been the one they had seen in the photograph album back at the Tower. With no time to lose Fred and Charlie took to the skies and, as Belvedere studied the map that had now returned to the back of the clue once again, they headed for Madame Tussaud's.

5
chapter

The grand tour of Madame Tussaud's

Although Fred, Charlie and Belvedere did not need to arrive at Madame Tussaud's too early, they wanted to make sure that they were there in good time. Their first clue was beginning to play on their minds and excitement was building. Belvedere had already started work, trying to solve the clue whilst he bounced around in his satchel as Charlie banked this way and that, trying to avoid lampposts and buildings. The ones with satellite dishes were the ones you had to take care of.

The little Gronk was very grateful for the hole that Charlie had made. Below he could see all the traffic and people going about their business. All they needed now was some form of communication whilst they were in flight and Belvedere could direct Fred and Charlie from inside the satchel. Hopefully they would find something on their travels. In the meantime Belvedere had to concentrate on solving the clue.

The weather, so far, had been very good. If it had been raining, the satchel would have become far too heavy for Charlie to carry and that would have delayed them. But, as it was, they were making very good time and, as Fred and Charlie flew round a corner, there before them stood the big green dome of Madame Tussaud's. Flying closer, Fred and

Charlie could hear the crack of the flags that hung from the front of the building as they fluttered in the wind.

Fred and Charlie became very nervous, as it was obvious that they would have to fly through the flags and land. One false move and they were certain to crash into the flagpoles or worse, be trapped in one of the flags. Just then without warning a flock of pigeons flew in front of Fred and Charlie.

"'Evening," shouted the pigeons as they flew on their way, not caring that they could have caused an accident. Charlie shook his head in disbelief. Was it possible that pigeons could be so stupid?

Fred, however, was a lot more angry than Charlie and shouted after the pigeons, "Air Hogs, why don't you watch where you are going?"

"It's no good, Fred, they can't hear you," said Charlie who was now concentrating on where they could land safely. Belvedere was a little shaken up from the sharp turn Charlie had taken to avoid colliding with the pigeons and once again began to worry about the landing they were about to make. As they circled round Baker Street tube station there was a bustle with many Rucksacks rushing about. Fred, however, was more interested in the many cars that were waiting at the traffic lights. Then, all of a sudden, Fred stuck out his feet and lowered his wings stopping in mid air. He had seen the car of his dreams. It was sparkling in the evening sun and, as it gracefully pulled away, Fred noticed in silver the words

JAGUAR XKR. If only ravens could drive, he thought, then that would be the car for him. Charlie, who had had no interest in cars, called back to Fred for him to catch up, and as Fred's car disappeared into the distance, he caught up with Charlie.

Gently the two brothers began their descent having decided on a sensible landing spot. To their relief Fred and Charlie touched down on the roof of Madame Tussaud's without a problem. Charlie removed the satchel whilst Fred sat down gazing into the sky, obviously still dreaming of his car.

"At last. I thought we were going to have another rough landing, but well done, not a bump or a slip," said Belvedere, climbing out of the satchel rubbing his eyes, slightly blinded by the evening sun. The little Gronk looked ruffled and Fred noticed a tiny piece of his hair was sticking out from under his hat, which made him chuckle. Charlie turned to see what Fred was laughing at and as he looked at Belvedere he too began to chuckle. Belvedere however did not see what was so funny.

"I don't know what you two are laughing at. You should try sitting in that satchel as you two attempt to fly."

Charlie raised his beak into the air and simply said, "You are flying with the best pilots in the raven air command, I will have you know. We trained at Top Fun, the best training ground in the world for pilots."

Fred and Belvedere began to laugh as Charlie pulled a pair of mirror sunglasses from his jacket and placed them on the end of his beak. So that Belvedere understood what Charlie was talking about, Fred whispered into his ear that his brother had been watching too many films. Belvedere agreed and, whilst Charlie sat back trying to look impressive with his glasses on the end of his beak, Belvedere laid out some sandwiches as he was certain Fred and Charlie must be hungry after all the flying they had done. As Belvedere passed round the sandwiches the three of them discussed how they were going to get inside to try and find Doc Curtious.

Full up and rested, Fred, Charlie and Belvedere knew it was time for them to make a move. They had decided the best way in was to slide down one of the flagpoles and try to find an open window. Charlie was the first to slide down the pole and found it very difficult to get a grip. He slid down faster than he had intended, landing at the bottom with a bump. Fred followed and equally found it difficult to get a grip. Like his brother he slid down the pole faster than he would have liked.

Fred and Charlie laughed as they rubbed their sore bottoms. Belvedere who had landed quite softly saw the amusing side of Fred and Charlie hopping about rubbing their tail feathers. Amongst all the laughter Charlie pointed out that they really were rather stupid, as they should have flown down, which made every one laugh even more. Finally the laughing stopped and Fred noticed a tiny door at the end of the ledge. As they walked along the edge of the building Fred and Charlie hoped that it was open. In no time at all the three of them found themselves at the tiny door. Belvedere seemed very excited at the prospect of seeing if the door was open. As Fred raised his wing to try the door, Charlie stopped him.

"Wait. We do not know who is on the other side, Remember, Tibbs told us to be careful. Mustafat could be waiting to catch us."

Silence fell. They had forgotten about the dangers that they had been warned about. Neither of them wanted to end up victims of Mustafat's paws. Charlie took a step back as did Belvedere. Fred thought for a while and then without a word stepped forward and knocked on the door, but there was no reply. Slowly Fred tried the door handle to see if it would open and, to his surprise, it began to turn. As quiet as a mouse he opened the door an inch at a time, revealing only darkness within.

Charlie removed his Swiss army knife from the satchel and jammed it in the door so it would not slam shut and trap them inside. Fred and Belvedere were surprised at the intelligence behind what Charlie had just done. Beaming from ear to ear, Charlie explained he had seen it in a film once. Now with the door wide open Belvedere spoke aloud.

"Well, now it is open, one of us has got to go inside and seeing that you two are bigger than me I suppose it has to be me."

Not giving Fred and Charlie the chance to argue, not that he thought they would, Belvedere entered the darkness through the door. Fred and Charlie waited in silence and as the minutes ticked by they became more and more anxious. Suddenly Belvedere appeared at the door with a smile beaming across his face, much to the relief of Fred and Charlie.

"It is brilliant in here, you should see it. Charlie, you will love it. There are film stars, in fact, everyone that is famous."

The word film star was too much for Charlie. He pushed his way past Fred and followed Belvedere into the darkness and into Madame Tussaud's. Fred removed the Swiss army knife and looked around to see if anyone was watching them, then he too entered the darkness, closing the tiny door behind him.

Once inside, and their eyes had become accustomed to the darkness they could see wax models of people sitting and standing. They were so lifelike. Charlie could not believe his luck. Of all the places they could have ended up, here he was amongst all the stars he had idolised since a young raven. As Fred and Belvedere began to explore Charlie rushed about muttering and gasping at the same time.

"No Doc Curtious then, Belvedere," said Fred, taking great care not to knock into anything.

"Not yet, but with the noise Charlie is making some one will soon turn up."

Fred agreed and read out loud a plaque that he had found.

"THE GARDEN PARTY."

Rubbing his beak in confusion, Fred looked about the room and realised that it had been set out as an English garden. Very clever, he thought, as he followed Belvedere who was trying to keep an eye on Charlie. Each model they passed seemed so lifelike. Nigel Mansell, the great British racing driver who won the formula one championship in 1992. Dudley Moore, a fine English actor, best known for his role in Arthur which won an Oscar nomination. Charlie was now standing in front of Dudley bowing. Fred was concerned that Charlie might have gone mad with all the excitement. As they moved about the room they passed even more celebrities; Nick Faldo, the golfing legend, Lenny Henry, Bob Hoskins and of course the world famous Elizabeth Taylor. Then Fred and Charlie noticed that Belvedere had stopped and was pointing at one of the wax models.

"Look, I wonder if he is a relative."

The little Gronk was pointing at a tiny man who only stood four inches high. Fred noticed that to the side of the little man was a plaque with some writing on it. Fred cleared his throat and read aloud, "Tom Thumb, born in 1838. His real name was Charlie Stratton and he was only forty inches high. Tom Thumb liked to dress as Napoleon. There is no mention that he was a Gronkiedoddle, Belvedere. So I don't think he is a relative."

Belvedere stood and thought for a while, whilst Fred and

Charlie looked around some more. Before long Belvedere's thoughts were disturbed by the silence that had fallen about the room. Fred and Charlie were not making a sound, and this worried Belvedere. Looking around he noticed that the two brothers were standing in front of a wax model. As he walked over to them he noticed that Fred and Charlie were looking very nervous.

"What's wrong with you two?" questioned the little Gronk. Fred and Charlie pointed at the wax model. Just then a voice came from behind them. Fred and Charlie jumped into the air with fright and Belvedere ran off to hide behind the feet of the world's greatest Sumo wrestler, Chiyonogugi, better known as Wolf. This was the model that Fred and Charlie had been pointing at.

"Ah ha, bonjour, glad to meet you, I am so happy you have arrived safely," came the voice again. This time Fred and Charlie could see a large poodle dog had appeared from the darkness of one of the corners. The large poodle was covered in paint, and what looked like wax.

"Ah, I am sorry, I did not mean to scare you. Please accept my apologies. My name is Doc Curtious, the finest French poodle in the whole of London. You see Madame Tussaud was taught the art of wax model making by my father's, father's master, and I have been a friend of the Tussaud family for many years. That is why at night I wander around this vast building making sure that all is well and the models are kept in good working order. They have to look their best you know.

Anyway, The Great Gob sent me word that you might be coming as I believe that you have to solve a clue, is this not correct, mes amis!"

Fred and Charlie were amazed at the Doc's accent. They had never heard anyone speak like he did before. Fred decided to step forward and introduce himself and his brother, not forgetting Belvedere.

"EnchantÈ, mes amis. Welcome to Madame Tussaud's, the world-famous attraction, here in London and Amsterdam. Belvedere, a Gronkiedoddle, what a pleasure it is to meet you. We have many Gronkiedoddles in Paris. I presume they are relatives of yours?"

Belvedere agreed that they probably were, and shook Doc Curtious by the paw. Fred, Charlie and Belvedere chatted with Doc Curtious for quite some time before finally with a snap of his paw he told them to follow him into the world of Madame Tussaud's.

In a much brighter area Doc Curtious asked to see the clue. Charlie produced the card on which the riddle was written whilst Fred and Belvedere looked at all the parts of the wax models that now surrounded them in glass cases. Doc Curtious, before reading the clue, explained that in this part of Madame Tussaud's it explained how they made the models and brought then to life with real hair, clothes and special effects. Doc Curtious read the clue out loud.

IN THE TRUE SPIRIT OF LONDON
YOU WILL FIND YOUR FIRST CLUE
ATTACHED TO THE CHEST OF A PIGEON
DRESSED IN RED WHITE AND BLUE

"AH HA," exclaimed Doc. "I might be able to help you. We have a ride inside this very building called 'The Spirit Of London'. It is there that you will find your next clue I am sure."

Fred and Charlie were amazed. Could this mean that in a matter of hours they could be on their way to the second attraction? Belvedere, who was equally excited, jumped about and did the most impressive back flip. Charlie simply muttered that he, too, could do that, much to everyone's amusement.

The clue now made sense and, as the Doc led the way through a large door that led to where all the very famous kings and queens - not forgetting politicians - were kept, everyone concerned was unaware that behind them a shadow of a cat was following them.

Back at the Tower of London all seemed to be returning to normal after the great excitement of Fred, Charlie and Belvedere leaving on their great adventure. Hector dozed as usual, whilst Bostrum and Honourous played chess in the corner of Hector's office. The pigeons were keeping an eye out for Lucif, and Ripper kept a close eye on the pigeons with Sweeney and Todd at his side.

"Well Ripper, what are we going to do now? You want to get your hands on the book 'The Great London Adventure' and hold the title as Grand Master of all the animals, and we are prepared to help you. But we need to have a plan. So far all we seem to be doing is sitting about, so what is the plan?" questioned Sweeney. Ripper who had been deep in thought turned and tapped his fellow companion on the head with the end of his wing. The smile that beamed across Ripper's face was the most evil smile Sweeney and Todd had ever seen. It sent shivers down their spines and, as Ripper told them to move closer, they felt very scared.

"Now listen to me, you pair of oily rascals. There is only one way that we will get our hands on that book and snatch the title for me, and that is to steal it."

Sweeney and Todd looked at each other as if to say 'well that is obvious', but without questioning this, they allowed Ripper to continue. "I have heard a rumour that Fred, Charlie and Belvedere are heading towards Madame Tussaud's. So whilst I am doing my pitiful duties here, I want you two to fly over there and see what they are up to. This will give me time to think and make some more plans. Once you have located them, report back to me and I shall tell you what to do next."

Sweeney and Todd agreed with the plan. However, unknown to them in the roof space below them four kestrels sat listening to Ripper's plans. Buster, Duster, Tickle and Polish, the four kestrels, were very concerned about the conversation they had just overheard.

"Well, we can't just sit here and allow Ripper to get away with that. AGHHH, I would love to bend that beak of Ripper's, I never have liked him," said Buster all of a flutter, trying very hard to keep his grip on the beam as he rustled his feathers.

"Now, Buster, you can't sort everything out with a rough and tumble. Sit back down and behave yourself," ordered Polish, who was busy dusting a corner of their house. As Buster sat down, a little embarrassed about his outburst, Tickle burst into laughter.

"Ha ha ha ha ha ah. Why don't we tell Hector? Ha Ha Ha Ha."

"No way. You know what happened the last time we told him some news. Remember when Eugene stole our lunch, what did Hector keep saying? Never in a hundred years. And lo and behold, Eugene has been sent to Wales for stealing Hector's feathers and attacking Rucksacks. No, this time we will have to sort it out for ourselves," explained Duster, sweeping up after Polish. Buster suddenly leapt to his feet again, this time hitting his head on the roof and knocking Tickle and Polish off the beam.

"I have got it. Why don't we wait until Fred, Charlie and Belvedere return from the quest and, if Ripper tries to capture the book or them, we grab hold of him. We then hold him captive up here until the ceremony is over and Fred, Charlie and Belvedere are crowned Grand Masters of all the animals."

"BRILLIANT," shouted the others. Buster was so happy that he had suggested something useful that he leapt up into the air once again striking his head against the roof. Polish, who was also so pleased that they had found a solution, suggested that they had a good old fashioned singsong and in no time at all the four kestrels were singing at the top of their voices. Ripper, who was still sitting above them, wondered what all the noise was about. Little did he know it was about him!

As the kestrels sang out loud Ripper tried to concentrate on his plans. Unable to think clearly, Ripper was forced to move to another rooftop leaving the kestrels to their singing.

Fred, Charlie, Belvedere and Doc Curtious had to move very quickly as the Garden Room where they had first met was now filling up with people. The Doc explained that very often they used the room for private functions. Well, where better than to have a party than amongst the stars? As they all made their way quietly into the next room Charlie suddenly flung his wings into the air, almost knocking Doc Curtious off his feet.

"Fred, Fred, Belvedere, LOOK. All my favourite stars under one roof, Oh, Oh look, there is Michael Caine and Joan Collins, fine actress her, you know. OH WOW, Eddie Murphy, this is too much."

Fred could not believe that Charlie was actually getting the names right, he seemed to be in a world of his own. Fred's amusement at his brother's excitement was not to last. The silhouette of the mystery cat had returned, but this time both Fred and Doc Curtious saw it.

"Did you see that, mes amis," Doc Curtious whispered into Fred's ear. Even Belvedere had noticed the shadow and looked up at Fred who was nodding to Doc. Fred looked over at Charlie, who was unaware of the possible danger and was studying James Bond, 007. Slowly the shadow could be seen to be creeping behind the models. It was time to move on and quickly, thought Fred. Grabbing Charlie by the wing Fred hurried away, but Charlie, still unaware that something was wrong, just kept talking.

"The name is Charlie, Charlie Bond. 007 to my friends."

Fred stopped and explained to Charlie that someone or something, possibly a cat, was following them and to hurry up. Charlie did not need to be told twice that someone or something was following them, he was gone. Fred was certain he turned a funny shade of white. Charlie entered the next room at such speed he made one of the models spin round.

Once everyone was in the large room they had just entered they all felt happier. It would be very difficult for anyone or anything to creep up on them. Convinced that the shadow was a cat, Belvedere was most concerned. After all a cat could swallow him whole. A shudder ran through Belvedere's body at the thought of the fishy breath. As Doc Curtious continued with his tour everyone kept very close indeed. The Doc explained each model as they moved past.

"Now this here is William the First, King of England and the models go right the way through to our present day Queen. This is the largest room in Madame Tussaud's and very popular."

Belvedere thought that The Great Gob should be in this room, but decided not to say anything. Suddenly without warning Doc Curtious stopped and began searching through his pockets.

"Ah ha, I nearly forgot. This is for you, so that you will never forget you visit here."

Doc Curtious handed Belvedere a very old piece of paper that looked like parchment. He explained that it was the family tree of the Royal family naming all the kings, queens that had ruled over Britain and their children. The three adventurers could not believe their eyes. The old parchment on which many names were written must have dated back many years. Belvedere carefully placed it in Charlie's satchel. Fred, Charlie and Belvedere thanked Doc Curtious and told him that whenever they looked at it they would think of him.

The Doc seemed to blush, but it was very difficult to tell with all his white fur. Taking great care and having a good look around, they continued on their tour. The one place, however, that no one thought to check was the ceiling above them and as they once again began to make their way through the attraction a pair of green eyes watched from high above their heads.

With each step that Fred, Charlie, Belvedere and Doc Curtious took they felt certain someone was watching them. Then, all of a sudden, they all heard a strange noise. Stopping without a word, they waited. From the darkness someone sneezed.

Charlie was the first to flee, followed closely by the others. The faces of Winston Churchill, Bill Clinton, Mikhail Gorbachev, Nelson Mandela and Bob Geldof flashed by. There was no time to stop and admire the wax models now. Without warning Charlie came to an abrupt stop. Fred and Doc Curtious crashed into him, wondering what was wrong. Fred, noticing that Belvedere was out of breath, placed him in the satchel for safety and speed, should they have to make a quick escape. But why had Charlie stopped?

"Look, Fred, my all time favourite band, the Bugs."

"Charlie, it is not the Bugs, it is the Beatles. Now, will you please get a move on?" shouted Fred, annoyed that Charlie had stopped over a band. Then, behind them, they all heard a loud thud. It sounded like something falling to the floor, like a cat! Not wanting to find out, once again they took to their heels, but not for long. This time it was Doc Curtious who stopped abruptly.

"What is it now?" questioned Fred, concerned that the sound of heavy paws on the carpet was growing closer by the second. Doc Curtious turned to the others with a worried look on his face.

"You see those stairs? They lead to the Chamber of Horrors, and we have to go down them in order to get to the Spirit Of London ride. I have heard some terrible stories about what happens down there. I have never even dared enter..."

Doc Curtious allowed the statement to hang in the air. But they all knew they had no choice. It was either the darkness of the Chamber of Horrors or capture by the cat that was now too close for comfort. On tiptoe and without a sound Fred, Charlie and Doc Curtious descended the dark cavernous stairs that lay ahead. Belvedere watched from the hole in the side of the satchel. As their eyes became used to the dull lighting they found that they had been transported back into Victorian times, in fact to a Victorian street, outside a public house called The Ten Bells, to be precise. All that could be heard was Charlie's beak chattering.

"Oh no, this is what I was afraid of. I have heard about this place. This is where many years ago the famous killer, Jack The Ripper, stalked women before he murdered them. You know they never caught him and it was rumoured that he was part of the Royal family. But I never told you that. Come on, we had better move on."

Nobody said a word as they edged their way along the street, listening to every sound. Charlie kept as close to Fred as possible as he whispered in his ear.

"This Jack The Ripper. I wonder if he is any relation to Ripper back at the Tower?"

Fred, slightly annoyed that Charlie was not concentrating and keeping his eyes open for strange shadows, snapped at him. "Charlie, Jack the Ripper was human, not a raven. Ripper probably called himself after him to make himself sound as if they were related. Now, keep your eyes open."

Belvedere, who had heard Fred's stern words to his brother, lifted the satchel flap to see what was going on. He wished so much that they could return to the London that he knew.

As they pressed on down the cobbled street they could hear screams and noises of people. Both Fred and Charlie could feel their feathers sticking up in fright. Then, to their utter panic, the shadow of a cat could be seen behind the windows of The Ten Bells public house. The shadow looked to be ten feet tall. Fred, Charlie, Doc Curtious and even Belvedere cried out with all their might. They were not going to wait around any longer. Running was their only option and, as they fled down the cobbled street, they could hear the sniggering of a cat.

Out of breath, but determined not to stop, they turned a corner. Suddenly, behind a thick glass panel, a room lit up and a voice boomed at them, it seemed to come from every corner of the corridor they now stood in.

"Garry Gilmore is the name. I faced a firing squad in 1977."

This was no place for poodles, ravens or even Gronkiedoddles. As they once again began to run, voices boomed at them and faces appeared from the dark. Faces like Christie and George Joseph Smith. Finally they reached a flight of stairs that would lead them to safety, they hoped! Leaving behind them the chilling tales and activities of the Chamber of Horrors and its ten foot tall cat.

The climb up the stairs was a long and tiresome one, but the Doc explained that at the top was a café where they could rest and get a drink, if, that is, they were not followed. Once safely in the café Charlie let Belvedere out of the satchel and Fred flopped into a chair to rest his legs.

"Phew! I don't know about anybody else, but that Chamber of Horrors gave me the creeps," said Fred wiping a bead of sweat from his brow.

"No, No, No, No, I was not scared at all, not after all the horror films I have seen, but I wonder who that cat was. I was going to stop and ask him, but I did not want to leave you three alone."

Fred rolled his eyes. Charlie had been more scared than anyone else had, but he would never admit it. Doc Curtious returned with a tray of drinks. Placing the tray on the table, he uttered the words that Fred, Charlie and Belvedere did not want to hear.

"It has to be Mustafat."

Charlie's eyes stood out on stalks at the very thought. Nobody dared say a word. Mustafat, if it was him, had found them. Fred, Charlie, Belvedere and Doc Curtious had taken the easy route out of the Chamber of Horrors. For Mustafat it was not so easy and it was taking him a long time to find his way. What was concerning him even more now, was that he felt that someone was watching him and he had his paw caught in something.

Whilst the four adventurers caught their breath sipping the drink that Doc Curtious had very kindly made for them, Honourous and Bostrum were playing draughts back at the Tower. The crows'feather radio sat silent in the corner. It had been hours since any reports had come in regarding sightings of Fred and Charlie.

"I hope my boys and Belvedere are alright!" sighed Bostrum, taking two more of Honourous's pieces.

"Oh, I am sure they will be fine. I remember the time when I set out to earn the right of being Grand Master and the right to hold the book The Great London Adventure. Mind you, in those days the traffic was not as heavy and light pollution as it is today makes flying at night very difficult to the untrained eye, but I am sure they will be fine."

Bostrum agreed, although not one hundred percent convinced, and continued with their game of draughts. Meanwhile as the sound of draught pieces being moved filled Hector's office Ripper was on the roof making his evil plans.

Sweeney and Todd had returned after a quick flight over to Madame Tussaud's where they had been talking to a pigeon that claimed that he had seen Fred and Charlie enter. Ripper rubbed his wings with glee.

"Okay great, we know where they are. Now all the pigeons round here are terrified because of my little note on the wall. All I have to do is make sure Hector does not realise what I am doing or it would be the tar dump for me. But you are sure it was them entering Madame Tussaud's?"

Sweeney and Todd grinned at Ripper and produced a black raven feather. Ripper snatched the feather from Sweeney's wing and took a deep sniff with his beak.

"AHHH yes, it is them all right. Now all we have to do is keep an eye on them and make sure they finish this quest. Then once they are back at the Tower, all the power and knowledge they have earned will be mine and it will be the tar dump in Wales for them."

Ripper, Sweeney and Todd let out loud evil laughs. Below them Sledger was making his way to Hector's office, not that there was anything to report, all the ravens were on their best behaviour, but he just wanted to make sure that there was nothing he wanted him to do.

Ripper hurled seeds and shouted at Sledger as he walked below. But Sledger simply quickened his pace and ignored him. He did not want any more feathers plucked.

Refreshed and feeling a lot better, Fred, Charlie, Belvedere and Doc Curtious were now ready to continue and try and find the clue. Doc cleared away the glasses and wiped the table whilst Charlie secured Belvedere once again in the satchel.

Mustafat however was now feeling very tired and scared. He was lost and freeing his paw from a gap in the floor had taken him a long time. He wished his two associates Saber and Foil, were with him. Then to his delight he saw a sign that clearly read EXIT in big red letters. At last he was safe and could continue with his pursuit of the ravens.

Once in the café Mustafat knew he was close as he had found a black feather on the floor. He knew that there was only one place they could have gone and that was the Spirit of London ride. So he quickly left the café to try and regain lost time.

The Doc hurried Fred and Charlie along unconcerned that Belvedere might have a rough ride. Speed was very important if they were to escape the clutches of Mustafat. They ran into a room with a series of ramps that zigzagged their way down to a row of miniature black London taxis. Once at the taxi's Doc Curtious told them to touch nothing whilst he turned the power on. As Doc disappeared from sight Fred and Charlie climbed aboard one of the taxis and released Belvedere from the satchel.

In no time at all Doc Curtious had made his way to the electricity power supply that turned the Spirit of London ride on and, although he knew it was very dangerous to play with electricity, he knew he had to turn on the power to the ride. Finding the switches, Doc closed his eyes and with all his might switched the power on.

Turning round Doc Curtious froze. In front of him two large green eyes appeared. He knew that Mustafat had caught him, but he had to return to Fred and Charlie. What was he to do?

Mustafat edged his way forward until Doc Curtious could see him clearly.

"I want the ravens," hissed Mustafat with an evil scowl on his face. Not knowing what to do, Doc Curtious puffed up all his fur and let out an almighty bark and to his amazement Mustafat leapt into the air with fright and ran off into the dark.

Charlie, hearing the bark, leapt from the taxi, not knowing what he was really going to do. But no sooner had his feet left the taxi than they were back inside as the door that Doc Curtious had left by sprung open.

"I don't want to die, Fred. Tell Mustafat to leave us alone," whimpered Charlie. But there was no need to worry. Doc Curtious had opened the door and was now running towards the taxi. With a hop, skip and a jump the Doc jumped into the taxi and pressed the start button. The four of them were now on the Spirit of London ride.

Fred, Charlie and Belvedere were amazed at the ride. It was so exciting. Music played as the tiny taxi turned this way and that taking them back more than four hundred years into British history. Colourful jesters and minstrels surrounded Queen Elizabeth the First (1533 ñ1603), who took England into the golden age of discovery, and then they saw Sir Francis Drake, who defeated the Spanish Armada with his English fleet. Doc Curtious sat back and watched the excitement on Fred, Charlie and Belvedere's faces. This was a ride they would not forget. Doc Curtious leant forward and explained to his friends that not many animals had seen the ride so they were very lucky. But Fred, Charlie and Belvedere were more interested in what was going on then listening to Doc Curtious.

Onward they travelled, hearing about William Shakespeare (1564ñ1616). He wrote many classics such as Hamlet in the public house know as The Boar's Head. This way and that the ride jolted, now they were journeying through the Great Fire of London (1666) and as the ride moved along shouting could be heard from the baker.

"Everyone blames me."

The fire swept through London destroying houses, thirteen thousand to be exact. After five days Sir Christopher Wren was given the task of rebuilding London. On through the ride they travelled and each inch of the way was as captivating as the last. Until finally they reached a large merry-go-round, where music played and models danced. Then Fred suddenly leapt to his feet.

"Look, the clue, over there. It is the clue."

"I can see it," shouted Charlie. Doc Curtious leant out of the taxi as it passed a pigeon wearing a union jack vest and grabbed the clue. They had found it. The four of them cheered as the ride came to an end. Oh, how proud their father would be, thought Fred.

Quickly and very excited, they all hurried into the next room and left behind the Spirit of London ride, the best ride they had ever seen. But the room they were in was too dark to read the clue. Space suits surrounded them and mission control was talking in the background. Doc Curtious explained that this was part of the tour they would not have time for, but one day when they returned he would be happy to show them around. In the meantime they had better go into the souvenir shop where there was bound to be more light to read the clue.

Once inside the souvenir shop Belvedere told them to open the clue. He was so excited. Charlie, however, was more interested in all the gifts that lined the shelves. Fred opened the black envelope with a familiar gold crest on it and read aloud.

**NOW YOU HAVE FINISHED THE
RIDE IN SIGN-NOTE CONFIDE
A HUSH CAN BE FOUND TO THE
MONUMENT YOU ARE BOUND**

"Ah well, there you go. Another clue we cannot understand. I am sure that Honourous thinks these up. How on earth are we meant to know were to go now?" said Charlie, a little tired and fed up. Belvedere, however, was deep in thought. Suddenly he snapped his fingers together.

"I have it. A hush can be found to the monument you are bound. Of course, Whisper the Owl. He lives at the Royal Albert Monument outside the Royal Albert Hall. That's where we have to go."

Doc agreed with Belvedere. Whisper did live at the Royal Albert monument and Sign-Note was the conductor and headmaster of the Royal Order of Water Rats Music School. Whisper would be certain to know where to find him. Fred and Charlie patted Belvedere on the back. He had done a very good job.

Although happy about solving the clue, Fred, Charlie and Belvedere were sad that they had to leave Doc Curtious. He had become a good friend and they would return to visit him. After many hugs and exchanges of good luck, the three adventurers left Madame Tussaud's by a window that Doc Curtious had opened especially for them.

Once again up into the sky, Fred and Charlie flew with Belvedere peering out of his hole in the satchel. The two brothers paused for a moment and looked back, Doc Curtious was waving from the window and Fred and Charlie waved back. Madame Tussaud's had been there for two hundred years and Fred, Charlie and Belvedere were convinced it would be there for another two hundred years.

As Doc Curtious finally shut the window and went back to tending to his wax models, Fred and Charlie flew across the night sky of London. To the Royal Albert Monument they were bound.

6
chapter
The Royal Albert Hall

With each flap of the their wings Fred and Charlie noticed that the sky was lightening. The morning sun was rising. They had been at Madame Tussaud's all night, but it had seemed only a short time. Doc Curtious was still on Fred's mind as they flew closer and closer to the Royal Albert Monument.

Belvedere had given Fred and Charlie precise directions from the satchel. For the time being the dangers they had faced with Mustafat hot on their tails seemed long ago. Tired but determined, Fred and Charlie flew on. To keep their spirits up Fred had suggested they sing a song and so Fred, Charlie and Belvedere sang at the tops of their voices.

The wonderful architecture of London spanned out below them, new amongst old, which had obviously been very well planned. Before long Fred and Charlie noticed yet another magnificent dome that lay in the distance. This had to be the Royal Albert Hall as Belvedere had told them to look for a dome.

"This has to be it, Charlie." shouted Fred, not sure whether he was relieved or excited. Charlie agreed and Belvedere, poking his head out of the hole, confirmed that it was indeed the Royal Albert Hall and the Royal Albert Monument was situated just in front of the vast building. Fred and Charlie soared round the vast dome looking for the monument. Then, to their sheer delight, it stood before them. So tall, so wonderful, and so shiny with its gold paint sparkling in the early morning sun that was now rising in its full glory.

With their wings outstretched Fred and Charlie came in into land. As their claws touched down they discovered they had a problem. Neither of them could get a grip, the ground was too slippery. Belvedere instinctively knew that something was wrong and curled up into a tiny ball to prepare himself for the crash that was certain to happen.

Out of control and very scared, Fred and Charlie slipped about all over the place. Any onlookers would have been convinced that they were trying to skate. The fence that surrounded the monument now presented another problem. Either they tried to jump it or it would mean a certain painful stop to their landing. Unfortunately for Fred and Charlie the painful halt to their landing was their only option and as they closed their eyes they waited to hit the fence.

Fred was the first to hit the fence followed closely by Charlie. Stunned and in a lot of pain, the two brothers sat with their legs through the fence and their beaks resting on the top of the fence. Belvedere who had been thrown from the satchel gathered himself together. He was not amused.

"Confounded birds. Why have you not learnt how to land

properly? If we finish this quest alive, it should go down in the history books."

Upset that they hurt all over and their bottoms were now very wet Fred and Charlie looked up at the monument that towered above them. Some Rucksacks (tourists) that had decided to take an early morning walk laughed at Fred and Charlie. Fortunately Belvedere had ducked out of sight before he was seen. Once the coast was clear Belvedere walked over to Fred and Charlie looking very stern.

"You two, if we ever survive this quest, you are going to the RAF Museum at Hendon to learn how to land. Now, please, in the meantime, could you just take care?"

Fred and Charlie nodded, not wanting to upset the Gronkiedoddle any further by trying to defend themselves. As Fred and Charlie straightened their uniforms a large owl flew from out of nowhere and joined them.

The owl fluffed up all his feathers. Charlie, who thought he was being polite, copied the owl, which seemed to irritate him.

"BAHHHHH, What are you doing here? Go back to the Tower where you belong."

Bewildered by the curt greeting, Charlie stepped forward.

"I'll have you know I am a black belt in karate. I have watched all the Bruce Lee films, so just be careful."

The owl laughed and turned his back on Fred and Charlie. Just then Belvedere stepped out from behind Fred's legs.

"Excuse me, my name is Belvedere the Gronkiedoddle. Are you Whisper the Owl?"

Whisper turned round and a look of surprise filled his face. Whisper then placed a wing over his eyes in shame. He could not believe that he had been so stupid. "I am so sorry, Please forgive me, but I get a lot of travellers that land here." Whisper mopped his brow with his handkerchief, and was obviously very sorry about his rudeness.

Fred stepped forward. "It's okay Whisper. I am sorry that we did not warn you that we were coming, but we are in a hurry. We are on the quest of The Great London Adventure, a quest The Great Gob has set us, and the clue that we found at Madame Tussaud's has led us to you."

Whisper once again mopped his brow, and thought for a few seconds. "Of course. How silly of me. I have a note from The Great Gob saying you may drop by. Oh, I had completely forgotten about it. I tend to forget everything these days."

Whisper searched through his pockets and tried to find the note, but being the silly owl that he was, he had lost it. Sitting down on the steps of the monument, Whisper placed his head in his hands. Charlie placed a wing round Whisper's shoulder and told him not to worry. Fred, Charlie and Belvedere explained how they had found the clue at Madame

Tussaud's and how Doc Curtious had helped them. Whisper seemed most impressed that they had come so far in such a short time.

Meanwhile, in another part of London, Lucif, the master criminal of all the capital, had heard about the note that Ripper had written on the walls. Lucif was not very happy that someone, especially a raven, had used his name without his permission. Action would have to be taken and Ripper would have to pay for his stupidity. More importantly Lucif now knew about the quest and could see his chance of becoming Grand Master of all the animals and holding the book The Great London Adventure. All he had to do was work out how he would get his paws on the book and capture Fred, Charlie and Belvedere.

Lucif paced up and down in his hideaway deep in Kensington Gardens. Up and down he paced repeating the same words out loud. "Lucif, Grand Master. Ummm, rolls off the tongue, a title fit for me."

Unaware of the plans Lucif was making, the two brothers and Belvedere listened to Whisper who was telling them all about the Royal Albert Monument, where he lived.

"You see I moved here from the country, fancied a bit of city life. I loved it so much I decided to stay. Then I was offered this place by The Great Gob. He told me to look after it and that is what I try to do. You see Sir Giles Scott built the monument. It took him nearly twelve years to build. It is supposed to be a shrine dedicated to the public. Up there is Prince Ponders, a great place to sit and think. Each corner represents agriculture, manufacture, commerce and engineering. The four inner corners represent Europe, Asia, Africa and America. What I like, though, is that it is very close to the parks, so at night I can take off and find some old trees to sit and think in. Wonderful place. I am very lucky."

Fred nudged Charlie, who had dropped off to sleep. He was so tired after all the flying and the close escape from Mustafat's paws. Whisper, being the perfect host, said that they should fly up to his nest so they could rest. Belvedere once again climbed into the satchel and before long everyone was settled in Whisper's very comfortable nest.

Whisper's home was full of old books and photographs of old London. Charlie had collapsed on a bed of moss and was sound asleep. Fred and Belvedere relaxed and were grateful of the time to rest their aching bones. Before long Fred and Belvedere drifted off to sleep whilst Whisper kept watch. Whisper paced up and down looking this way and that. Then suddenly he noticed a commotion on the pavement outside the Royal Albert Hall. With a blink of his large eyes Whisper focused on what was going on. To his concern Mustafat was talking to his partners in crime, Saber and Foil.

"Right, you two! Ravens are out and about in London and we are going to capture them. Ever had raven pie? Wonderful, it is. Now, Saber, go and sharpen those tools of pain of yours. Foil, get some rope, so we can tie them up once we have captured them. I am going to go and beg some food from my master. We have a long day and night ahead of us, so let's get to it." Saber and Foil slapped their paws together and shouted 'Raven Pie' at the top of their voices.

Whisper could not believe his ears, and was thankful that his powerful hunting ears could still work. He looked over at his guests and did not have the heart to wake them, so he decided to prepare some food.

With all the food made, Whisper had excelled himself as he had prepared a banquet fit for kings. Now all he had to do was to wake Fred, Charlie and Belvedere. Taking an old feather that had fallen out a few days earlier, Whisper tickled Fred and Charlie's beaks, not forgetting Belvedere's nose.

"AHHHCHOOOOOO," sneezed Fred and Charlie together, followed by Belvedere. Whisper's awaking plan had worked. The three adventurers were now awake. Sleepy, but awake.

"I say, Whisper. What do you think you are doing? AhhhhChoooo," questioned Fred whilst sneezing at the same time. Charlie stretched his wings and Belvedere rubbed his eyes trying to focus.

"You have been asleep for most of the day, and I think now we need to make plans for the next stage of your journey. I have made some food for us all to eat whilst we discuss a problem that I think you may have."

Fred, Charlie and Belvedere settled down to eat around the makeshift table that Whisper had constructed out of some old bricks and a plank of old bark. He explained that he had read the clue and thought he could help, but more importantly they had to address the problem he thought they had.

"Whilst you were sleeping I overheard Mustafat, Saber and Foil talking down there." Whisper pointed to the Royal Albert Hall. Then with a ruffle of his feathers he continued. "Mustafat is the caretaker's cat at the Royal Albert Hall and he knows that place like the back of his paw. He is planning to capture you and make you into raven pie, and I dread to think what he is going to do with you, Belvedere. Mustafat, however, is not very intelligent. He is more of your petty criminal. Now, Lucif, he is the one you have to look out for. He is the criminal Master genius."

Fred and Charlie gulped at the thought of being made into raven pie and Belvedere was not happy either. But what were they to do? Whisper went on to explain that they had to enter the Royal Albert Hall as Sign-Note lived there as well. Ruffling through some old papers, the wise old owl found a map of the Royal Albert Hall and spread it out in front of them.

"Now then, these plans will show you a safe way into the building, but after that you are on you own. I cannot help you any more, other than keep look out up here. If I should see Mustafat or any of his friends, I will sound this alarm." Whisper let out a huge hoot and Fred, Charlie and Belvedere covered their ears.

The wise old owl then went on to explain that a concert was scheduled for that night and that many Rucksacks (tourists) would be there, but this also meant that Mustafat would be on duty. Fred, Charlie and Belvedere were now more frightened than they had been at Madame Tussaud's. Master Criminals, raven pie and an uncertainty for Belvedere meant that great care had to be taken. The secret door into the Royal Albert Hall would help and the three of them were grateful that Whisper had shown it to them, but once inside they would have to find Sign-Note without getting caught by Mustafat.

Down below them crowds of Rucksacks had already started to form orderly queues outside the entrances to the great building. There was no more time for plans or talking, it was time for them to take action and set out on their next stage of the quest, one that they were certain was not going to be as easy as the last.

Whisper said his farewells to Fred, Charlie and Belvedere and they thanked him for his hospitality and help. As the two brothers took to the air with Belvedere once again safely hidden in the satchel Whisper took up his position of guard. He felt so proud that he was helping the future Grand Masters of London.

Within minutes Fred and Charlie landed outside the secret door. From where they were standing they could see Whisper keeping a watchful eye. Belvedere climbed from the satchel and stood next to his friends.

"Oh, this reminds me of a film. The smell of fresh cut grass, an orchestra warming up below and wonderful feelings."

Fred and Belvedere just looked at Charlie. He would not be feeling so wonderful if Mustafat caught him, thought Fred, but decided not to say anything. Slowly and very quietly Fred turned the handle of the tiny secret door and, as they stepped inside onto a thin ledge, they could see many humans taking their seats. Quietly Fred, Charlie and Belvedere waited. They could not possibly make a move yet for they would be sure to be seen. Slowly the Royal Albert Hall filled with people and before long the lights dimmed and a very smart man walked onto the stage right below them. A huge applause went up and, as the man tapped his baton, the orchestra began to play. The music was wonderful.

As the orchestra played Fred, Charlie and Belvedere wondered what to do. They could not stay where they were. Then from the shadows to their right they heard a noise. Panic filled them. Surely it was not Mustafat!

Charlie placed the satchel round his neck in case he had to make a quick getaway. Belvedere who was inside wished he could see what was happening. Just then, as if from nowhere Sign-Note appeared, dressed in a fine dinner suit.

"Quick, you must come with me. We don't have much time.

Mustafat is on his way."

Charlie needed to hear no other words than Mustafat. Quickly he edged his way along the ledge, taking care not to fall, Fred followed taking care not to hurry Charlie. Sign-Note showed Fred and Charlie into a small room. Sign-Note explained that they would be safe here as long as they did not make a sound and that he would return once he had made sure Mustafat was not around. With the door to the tiny room tightly shut Belvedere felt that it was safe for him to climb out of the satchel. Below them the applause of the crowd shook the floor where they were sitting, followed shortly by the noise of everyone leaving.

Sign-Note returned as he said he would, but Fred, Charlie and Belvedere felt that days had passed, although in truth they had only been waiting about half an hour. Sign-Note introduced himself to Belvedere and explained that he had scouts out looking for Mustafat, so should he appear they would have plenty of notice. The little water rat told Fred and Charlie to follow him closely and to keep Belvedere in the satchel, and with that scurried from the room. Belvedere once again climbed into the satchel and Fred and Charlie followed Sign-Note as quickly as they could. Once outside the little room Sign-Note had climbed down some steps and was waiting for Fred and Charlie to catch up.

"Come on quickly, we don't have time to wait around," hurried Sign-Note. The two brothers quickly found their step and were soon standing next to Sign-Note on the main stage at the Royal Albert Hall. All the seats were completely empty and rubbish was scattered everywhere.

"Now you can really see how big this place is," said Sign-Note gesturing with his arm to the massive dome above their heads. Fred and Charlie were amazed at such a beautiful place. Belvedere, who was now standing on one of the seats, whistled. Fred and Charlie thought of Janous and how much she would enjoy singing on the stage in front of hundreds of ravens. Fred and Charlie sat next to Belvedere as Sign-Note explained all about the building.

"It took six million bricks to build this place, quite a task in 1867, which was when the first brick was laid."

But Sign-Note knew that he could not spend all night explaining the history of the building, so, with a clap of his hands, what seemed to be hundreds of Water Rats, all carrying instruments joined him on the stage. With everyone in his or her places, Sign-Note raised his little arms and silence fell. It was time for him to address Fred, Charlie and Belvedere.

"My Lords, Ladies and Gentlemen, we are gathered here this night to welcome Fred, Charlie and Belvedere, for they have been chosen for The Great London Quest. But before you learn of your next clue, whatever it may be, we will play for you a collection of songs and classics, so that you can leave with the knowledge of music in your hearts."

A cheer rang out from the orchestra and everyone began to clap. Sign-Note took a bow in front of Fred, Charlie and Belvedere before turning to his orchestra. Then, with a tap of his baton, the music began.

As Sign-Note moved his arm this way and that, the music continued. So fantastic was the concert that Fred, Charlie and Belvedere had not seen Sign-Note's guards climb high up above their heads to keep watch. Peeper and Eyeball, the guards in question, were now walking along the top of the organ pipes, some ten thousand of them, behind the orchestra. This was a perfect look-out for them. They could see everything from up there, including a pair of green eyes that was watching the proceedings. That could mean only one thing - Mustafat and trouble with a capital T.

Peeper tried to whistle to Eyeball, but he could not hear over the music. But Eyeball was an experienced guard and he had already spotted the green eyes in the darkness at the back.

Mustafat, who had now climbed with Saber and Foil up onto a railing three stories above the stage, right at the back, was licking his lips. Mustafat signalled to Saber and Foil and pointed to where Fred, Charlie and Belvedere were sitting below. Peeper and Eyeball had to act quickly if they were to save the three guests. There was no time to lose. They grabbed hold of the curtain ropes that hung each side of the pipes and, as they swung out and down, the curtains closed, bringing the music to an abrupt end.

Fred and Charlie leapt into the air with fright as Peeper and Eyeball flew through the air. Mustafat, Saber and Foil seized their chance and dived from the balcony only missing Fred, Charlie and Belvedere by a whisker. Belvedere, being so small, had hidden in one of the air vents at the side of the stage.

"This is leader one to leader two. Let's get airborne," shouted Charlie to Fred as the commotion began to grow. The orchestra fled in many different directions and Saber and Foil had turned their attentions to Peeper and Eyeball. Sign-Note, who had taken refuge under a seat, poked his nose out to see what was going on, only to get it scratched by Mustafat. Fred and Charlie looked at the mayhem below and knew they had to do something before someone got really hurt.

"This is leader one to leader two, we have bandits at two and four o'clock, okay, chaps, let's take them out."

"Oh, shut up, Charlie," shouted Fred, concerned that his brother did not fully understand the danger that lay ahead in this combat situation. With the elegance of a great Spitfire Fred and Charlie banked round and dived down to Saber and Foil.

Success first time. Fred and Charlie now had hold of Saber and Foil by the scruffs of their necks and were lifting them high into the dome of the building. Saber and Foil scrambled to get a grip, but there was nothing to get a grip on as they were in mid air.

144

"On the count of three, Charlie," ordered Fred, as Charlie banked round and now faced his brother.

"Hey, Fred, we look like the Red Arrows up here," chuckled Charlie. The brothers flew towards each other only leaving it seconds before they banked away from a head on collision, letting go of Saber and Foil, who collided in mid air. Very stunned, Mustafat's helpers fell to the floor. This only left one problem for Fred and Charlie - Mustafat!

Shocked that Saber and Foil had failed him and by what Fred and Charlie had done to them, the now very angry Mustafat stood on his back paws shaking a paw at Fred and Charlie.

"I will get you, see if I don't," shouted Mustafat before running off through one of the many exits, leaving Saber and Foil all alone, much to their disgust. Getting to their feet and still stunned, Saber and Foil followed Mustafat, not wanting to take another flight with Fred and Charlie.

Panic suddenly raced through Fred and Charlie. Where was Belvedere? Had he been captured? Had he become lost forever? Calling his name, Fred and Charlie noticed the little Gronk climbing from an air vent. Sign-Note, who held a handkerchief to his nose, came out from underneath his seat and Fred and Charlie flew down to join them.

"Phew, that was a close one. I dread to think what could have happened if Fred and Charlie had not used their flying skills. We all could been captured by Mustafat!" exclaimed Sign-

Note, his voice muffled by the handkerchief as he tried to ease the pain from Mustafat's scratch. Belvedere, who had scrambled into the satchel, returned with a plaster and placed it carefully on Sign-Note's nose.

Getting to his feet, Sign-Note clapped his tiny little paws once again, and all the other water rats came out from where they had been hiding. As everyone gathered around, Sign-Note began to speak.

"I would like to thank Peeper and Eyeball for their bravery here tonight, but I would also like to thank Fred and Charlie, who really saved us from the clutches of Mustafat and his two helpers. Three cheers for Fred and Charlie. Hip Hip Hooray."

Everyone cheered including Belvedere. Fred and Charlie became quite embarrassed, but Charlie, being his true self, soon became used to it and he started bowing. The cheering soon died down, but Charlie kept bowing, until Fred nudged him hard in his ribs. Charlie wanted to keep the cheering going and, ignoring his brother, placed a wing in his mouth and tried to whistle, but all that happened was that he looked very silly as a strange noise was all that came out.

It was at this point that Sign-Note produced a shiny silver disk from the inside of his jacket. Fred, Charlie and Belvedere looked at him and wondered what it was.

"This is called a CD (compact disc), and on here is you next clue. The next part of your quest is to find out where you can play it, and then you will be able to continue."

As Sign-Note handed Belvedere the disc so he could put it in the satchel for safe keeping, a door slammed shut at the back of the hall. Looking, up Peeper and Eyeball shouted at the tops of their voices.

"It's the caretaker. Mustafat has gone and told him we're in here. RUN."

No sooner had Peeper and Eyeball shouted 'caretaker' then the stage cleared of the water rats. Sign-Note shouted back 'Good Luck' to Fred, Charlie and Belvedere and disappeared down an air vent. Belvedere ran to the satchel and climbed in as Charlie placed it round his neck once again for flight. Turning to Fred, fear filled Charlie.

"There is no escape, Fred. How are we going to get out of here?"

"Don't worry, Charlie, I have a plan. Follow me." Fred took to the air, closely followed by Charlie.

"Now, listen to me, Charlie. We are going to fly straight up and no stopping. Fly faster than you have ever flown before, and hold on tight, Belvedere."

Charlie nodded to his brother and a muffled 'Okay' came from the satchel. Charlie hoped that Fred knew what he was doing. With a quick circle of the Royal Albert Hall for speed,

Fred and Charlie flew faster than they had ever done before. Fred could see the window that had been left open as he and his brother headed for it as quick as bullets. To make it through the window was going to require precision flying, but they had to do it.

"Through the window, Charlie, and don't stop."

"WOPPPPPEEEEEEEEE," shouted Charlie, who was very excited about the speed they were reaching. The two brothers shot through the open window, out into the safety of the night air. Charlie had been worried about the satchel getting caught, but all he had done was clip his wing on the way through. The loss of one feather was a small price to pay.

Charlie's clipped feather fell to the floor of the Royal Albert Hall. Picking it up, the caretaker looked at it with great interest and muttered under his breath. "A Royal Yeoman Raven. I wonder what he was doing here."

Tucking the feather in his pocket the caretaker began to sweep the floor. Mustafat, who had been watching, banged his paw in anger. He had hoped his master would have captured Fred and Charlie for him. Now he was left with only one choice. He had to pack his bags and follow the two ravens on foot with his helpers Saber and Foil.

With the danger behind them, Fred and Charlie landed outside on the steps of the Royal Albert Hall. Charlie opened the satchel and Belvedere fell out. The three adventurers sat for a while catching their breath. That had been a hard escape and a very close one. Now all they had to do was find somewhere they could play the CD!

Seeing that they had escaped, Whisper flew down to join his friends. Little did he know how close they had been to capture. Belvedere rose to his feet as Fred and Charlie chatted with Whisper, telling him all about Mustafat, Saber and Foil. To Belvedere's annoyance a piece of paper had blown along the street and covered him from head to foot. It stuck to him like glue, one of the problems of being so small. Trying not to laugh, Fred and Charlie helped Belvedere untangle himself. Poor Belvedere was in such a state and very annoyed.

Sitting down once again, Fred and Charlie thought very hard where they could play the CD. Belvedere, however, was reading the piece of paper that had wrapped itself round him only a few minutes earlier. Suddenly he let out a shout.

"I have got it. Look, this leaflet is from Rock Circus at the Pavilion in Piccadilly. They will have a CD player there, I am sure they will."

The two brothers and Whisper agreed and once again Belvedere got a pat on the back. He really was a clever little Gronk.

With no time to lose and with the continuing threat of Mustafat, Fred, Charlie and Belvedere set off for Rock Circus, not forgetting to say a special thank you to Whisper for all his efforts and for guarding them so well.

Piccadilly was not that far, but Fred and Charlie decided to take it easy. Their bones ached from their escape and the satchel seemed to be getting heavier. With the night air rustling their wings, Fred and Charlie once again set off to continue on their quest.

7

chapter

The Rock Circus experience

The flight to Rock Circus in Piccadilly became harder as dark clouds had formed and rain had began to fall. The clothes Bascer, the raven tailor, had taken so much care over were now beginning to get heavy and flying was becoming a struggle. Even Fred and Charlie's claws had become blue with cold. Belvedere, however, was quite snug and warm in his satchel, but he felt sorry for Fred and Charlie.

"Not far now, Charlie," shouted Fred to his brother, concerned that the satchel would become too heavy and they would have to land.

"I hope this Rock Circus has some heating, so we can dry off," shouted Charlie, now drenched through and with rain falling from the end of his beak. Time was running out. In a few hours daylight would break and they would have to find somewhere to rest. The traffic seemed quite picturesque with the headlights reflecting off all the shop windows and the spray from the cars creating a fine mist. Then, as Fred and Charlie banked round a corner, to their relief the lights of Piccadilly lay ahead.

Rock Circus was not hard to find even in the rain. Outside, on the window ledge overlooking Piccadilly, a few of the Rock

Circus wax models stood, looking very wet but nonetheless very impressive. Above them a large neon light shone. They had found Rock Circus. Now all they had to do was find a way inside the building and try and dry off.

Fred and Charlie decided that the balcony underneath the neon sign was the best place to land and with the greatest of ease the two brothers touched down, with no complications. The two brothers collapsed in a heap whilst Belvedere scrambled from the satchel. He was so impressed with Fred and Charlie. It had been a hard flight for them and at the end they had managed to land safely.

Belvedere, who was very dry because he had been in the satchel all the time, pulled from the satchel a brightly coloured umbrella. With very little effort the little Gronk opened the umbrella and held it so that it kept the rain from falling on Fred and Charlie. It was the very least he could do. Happier that his travelling companions were at least sheltered, the little Gronk looked up and down the balcony for an open window or a doorway. Then, as he peered down to the traffic, below he let out a cry.

"Oh no! Oh my! Oh deary, deary me!" cried Belvedere. Fred and Charlie looked over to the Gronk and asked what he could see.

"Look, down there, by that record shop, Tower Records. It's Mustafat and the two cats he had with him at the Albert Hall. How did he get here so fast? He does not have wings."

Fred and Charlie got to their feet and joined Belvedere who was still looking over the balcony. Sure enough Mustafat and his helpers Saber and Foil were standing by the record shop. A taxi screeched to a halt as they made a dash across the road. There was no mistake though, it was Mustafat, Saber and Foil.

"Quickly, we have to get inside, before he sees us."

Out of breath after their near escape with the taxi, Mustafat, Saber and Foil looked about for any signs that ravens might have passed that way. Mustafat paced up and down in frustration. He knew that they had to be in the area, one of the water rats that he had captured earlier that evening had told him, so where were they?

Suddenly Mustafat froze to the spot. Saber and Foil were waiting for their orders from a puzzled Mustafat. Then a voice from the shadows could be heard, this time loud enough for Saber and Foil to hear.

"Not a very nice night to be wandering about the city, even for cats that look like drowned rats, ha ha ha ha ha ha."

The voice and laugh that came from the shadows sent shivers down Mustafat's spine. Mustafat slowly took a step forward into the dark shadows of the doorway and was confronted by a fox that was dressed in a leather jacket and leather trousers.

"Looks to me like you could do with somewhere to dry off. All three of you are soaked to the skin, and this rain is going to keep on falling, maybe for the rest of the day," said the fox, once again sending shivers down Mustafat's spine. Stepping even closer, Mustafat took a closer look at the fox. Saber and Foil, however, kept their distance in case they had to make a quick getaway.

"Who are you, and what are you doing here?" questioned Mustafat, trying to put on a deep voice. The fox stepped out from the doorway and held out his paw for Mustafat to shake it, but, to Mustafat's horror, there was no paw, simply a silver hook. Mustafat, now very unsure of the fox, shook the hook.

"The name is Flavel, the rebel without a paw."

Again a shiver shot down Mustafat's back, as he introduced himself, Saber and Foil. Not wanting to show his fear, Mustafat went on to explain that he was looking for two ravens that had been heading this way, in fact he knew that they were heading to Rock Circus. The fox laughed out loud and Saber and Foil took another step back. What was so funny they thought?

"This Rock Circus you talk about is over there. But if I were you, I would not venture inside. You see there is a very large dog that looks after the place at night and with only a few hours to go before morning he would love to find three cats. If these ravens you talk about have ventured inside, then chances are they are in his clutches right now, never to be seen again."

Saber and Foil did not like the sound of meeting a big dog at all. Mustafat equally swallowed hard at the thought of coming face to face with a dog. He had been caught once before and never talked about what had happened, but everyone that knew him was convinced that it could not have been pleasant. Flavel, noticing the three cats' concern, suggested that they might follow him home for a nice cup of hot milk and to give them a chance to dry off. Mustafat immediately agreed, but Saber and Foil were not so sure. They had been warned when they were kittens never to go off with a stranger and here was Mustafat agreeing to do just that.

Flavel assured Saber and Foil that it would fine and that they had nothing to worry about. So, after a lot of convincing, they agreed, but only on the condition that they took it in turns to wait outside his house so at least one of them could raise the alarm if needed. Mustafat, being older, equally assured them that he would take care of them.

So, as Mustafat, Saber, Foil and Flavel set off for a cup of hot milk and some warmth, Fred and Charlie had given up trying to open a round window high up on the balcony where they had landed. But, just then, as Charlie leant against the glass of the window, it spun round and he disappeared. Quickly Belvedere and Fred shot through the window before it closed locking them out. Fred had only just made it through in time before the window shut tight. Belvedere and Fred were standing on a desk but there was no sign of Charlie.

"Charlie, where are you? Are you all right?" whispered

Belvedere, concerned that if he shouted he might attract the attention of others. In the distance Fred and Belvedere could hear a muffled noise. There was very little light in the room, but as their eyes became accustomed to their dark surroundings they noticed that something was moving in the corner of the room. Belvedere, who had a tiny little torch in his pocket, took it out and turned it on. The sight that greeted them looked very funny, but both Fred and Belvedere resisted the temptation to laugh.

Charlie had landed upside down in a wastepaper basket. His feet were pointing up into the air and that was all that could be seen. As Charlie struggled to free himself the wastepaper basket began to topple and, with a clatter, Charlie and the contents of the basket rolled onto the floor. Getting to his feet Charlie raised a wing.

"Don't say a word, you two. I know it was silly. I know I could have been hurt, but I got us in, did I not? And in any case I knew exactly what I was doing." With that Charlie lowered his wing and Fred and Belvedere chuckled to themselves, but decided it was better not to say anything.

Belvedere shone his torch around the office. It was very similar to Hector's except the equipment was larger and newer. They had to find a way out and try and find somewhere they could play the CD. They had to hurry, however, as daylight was going to break soon and before long the place would be full of Rucksacks (tourists).

Mustafat was more concerned now as to where Flavel was taking them. The fox had brought them along the edge of a street and now stood in front of a very large set of gates, and in the road lined up were hundreds of motorbikes.

"I wish one of those was mine," said Flavel as he swung open the gates with a large hefty push.

"They belong to humans known as couriers, who deliver parcels all over London, dodging traffic all day, up this road and down that. What a life! Anyway this is my home, and it is the only garden in Wardour Street. That's the name of the street we have just come up, if you are interested," mumbled Flavel as he turned to look up and down the street. Then he gathered his new friends closer as if to tell them a secret.

"This street dates back many years. It is where they used to make violins, but don't tell Sign-Note at the Royal Albert Hall. Nowadays it is full of humans running up and down with silver brief cases and cans of film. I have been told it is the heart of the British film industry, but who knows?"

Mustafat, Saber and Foil did not know what to say, so they simply followed the fox inside the gates and he shut them with a loud clunk behind them. Once inside Flavel walked across the rich grass towards an archway that seemed to lead to a tunnel that went deep beneath the ground.

"Well, this is it, home sweet home. Bit of a squeeze to get inside, but once you are down there, it will be very comfortable and dry," explained Flavel before disappearing down the tunnel. Mustafat then took a step back.

"Okay, you two, you are meant to be my bodyguards. On you go, and check the place out."

Saber and Foil knew that one of them at least would have to go inside and check the coast was clear, so they decided to draw straws to see which. Saber lost and, much to his concern, he began to edge his way down the tunnel. Mustafat and Foil waited for Saber to return, and as time passed by, each second seemed to be an hour. Then, without warning, Saber's head popped out from the tunnel.

"It is fine, safe as houses. Flavel is a nice fox, no problems here. Foil, I know that we said one would stay outside, but trust me on this. We will be fine."

Foil and then Mustafat followed Saber down the tunnel. At the bottom Saber, Foil and Mustafat found themselves in a large room. The walls were covered in pictures of motorbikes and magazines were piled everywhere. The hot milk that Flavel had made sat steaming in engine pistons that were supposed to be mugs, and they sat on an old oil drum that was the coffee table. Saber and Foil sat down on an old torn settee leaving Mustafat the only option to sit in an equally old and torn chair. Flavel, who seemed not to care where he sat, pulled up an oil drum from the corner of the room.

"There now, that's better. You would have caught a chill if you had waited for your ravens out there much longer," said Flavel taking a long, loud sip of his hot milk. Mustafat, not wanting to seem rude, also took a sip, but to his horror the milk tasted of oil and he found it very difficult to swallow. Saber and Foil, however, enjoyed the unusual taste and drank theirs as fast as they could. To Mustafat's relief Flavel turned to check the wall clock, giving him just enough time to pour the hot milk into the plant pot beside him. Flavel, thankfully, had not seen Mustafat and, as he turned back, he once again began to talk in his deep and gruff voice.

" Now where was I? Oh yes, well you already know my name and I know yours, so I had better tell you a bit about myself. I have a brother, you know, who is very high up in the government. Don't like to talk about him much. All hush hush, you know. But, seeing that I am amongst friends, I may as well tell you. I was in the army, you see, Fox Trot RECCE to be precise, and well, I got caught trading rubbish bag secrets. Well, I mean, I had bills to pay and it was a quick way to make some money."

Saber and Foil suddenly began to feel very uncomfortable. Trading rubbish bag secrets was a serious offence and something they would not like to get involved in. As Flavel carried on with his story the two henchmen looked about for a quick exit. Mustafat, however, seemed engrossed in the tale and kept saying 'really' every time Flavel finished a sentence. Flavel, who seemed to be enjoying Mustafat's attention, carried on.

"You see, it was my brother that caught me trading the secrets. Well, we were disarming a snare at the time and they fell out of my pocket. Thought he would turn a blind eye as it were, but, no, he turned me over to the officers and of course they had to court-martial me. The decision was made to throw me out of the army and cut off my paw, so that is why I have a hook now." Mustafat urged the fox to continue. "Well, that's how I got this place. Perfect for me, you see, I have always loved motorbikes. Now I work for Lucif the master criminal of the whole of London, you see. I keep him posted about everything that is going on. He is not too bad to work for. Well, it pays the bills."

Mustafat's eyes stood out on stalks when he heard the name, Lucif. He had always been regarded as a small-time criminal cat, but if he could meet Lucif, well, that would make him a big-time cat amongst all the other cats. Wanting to know more, Mustafat asked if Flavel could introduce him to Lucif!

"Yes, no problem, I know him so well, he is like a brother to me," said Flavel, but Saber and Foil were not convinced and heard a certain hesitation in Flavel's voice. Mustafat was too interested at the prospect of meeting Lucif to notice anything, thought Saber, as he restlessly moved about in his seat. Flavel then suddenly looked about the room as did Mustafat and, as the two of them moved closer towards each other, Flavel began to whisper. "One thing I should mention. Don't ever mention the claw that is missing on his right paw. Lost that in Trickston Nick, the high security cats' prison. The story goes that Lucif made a dangerous escape and the claw is still stuck in the gates to the prison. One cat once dared to ask how he had lost it and was never seen again. So be careful what you say."

Mustafat agreed, and promised Flavel that he would never mention it. Sitting back on his oil drum, Flavel tapped his nose and nodded his head. Mustafat, not knowing what it meant did the same. Saber and Foil looked at each other in great concern, they knew that Mustafat's next question would be how he could meet Lucif. And sure enough it was. Flavel once again leant forward.

"What you would have to do is go to Kensington Palace gardens. There you will meet two large cats called Omph and Fisticuff. They will take you to Lucif, that I am sure. Just mention my name. But remember you had better have a good reason for wanting to meet with Lucif."

"Oh I do, Oh I do," shouted Mustafat, so excited that here he was talking big cat stuff with a fox. Looking about, copying Flavel's gesture earlier, Mustafat lowered his voice and sat even closer to Flavel.

"You see these ravens, well, they are no ordinary ravens. Oh no, they have a satchel. Could mean secrets from the Tower. So if Lucif and I become partners, he gets the satchel and I get the ravens. Simple."

An evil smile crept across Flavel's face. Lucif would be proud of him this time. Secrets from the Tower! Mustafat knew nothing of the quest that The Great Gob had set the ravens and the Gronkiedoddle. What a stupid Mustafat, thought Flavel. Lucif had been right, get Mustafat interested and he would capture Fred, Charlie and Belvedere for him and Lucif could take the glory of being Grand Master of all of London. Mustafat would be none the wiser.

As Flavel continued his stories, Fred, Charlie and Belvedere had found their way out of the office and to the door that led into the main area of Rock Circus. Belvedere pushed open the door with all his might taking care not to make too much noise. The room behind the door was very colourful and bright and in the centre was a large round stage filled with wax models, similar to what they had seen at Madame Tussaud's. Not making a sound the three adventurers watched as a large dog moved from model to model grooming and adjusting items of clothing.

The dog was wearing faded and torn jeans, a denim shirt and dark glasses. He was whistling out of tune and every now and then talking to the model he was attending.

"Well, Elton, time for your wash and brush up. It has taken me nearly two hours to sort Bob Marley's hair out, and let me tell you there is a lot of it. And Eric Clapton's guitar was so out of tune, a Rucksack must have been playing with it, but it sounds just fine now."

Just then Charlie noticed that Fred was beginning to fidget. It looked like he was going to sneeze, so his brother tried to place his wing under his beak to stop the sneeze, but it was too late.

"AHHHHHHHHHCCCCCHHHHHHHHHOOOOOOOOOOOO OOOOO," sneezed Fred very loudly. He must have caught a chill from all the rain, thought Belvedere, trying to keep out of sight as the dog must have heard such a loud sneeze. Charlie quickly stepped forward, giving Belvedere the chance to hide and Fred the time to blow his beak.

"Sorry about disturbing you, but my brother must have caught a cold. We are looking for the caretaker, perhaps you know where we might be able to find him?" said Charlie in his very best voice. The dog that had turned round to look at Charlie said not a word, but simply jumped off the stage and began to walk towards him.

"Get ready to run for it," whispered Fred out the side of his beak, hoping the hairy dog had not heard him.

"Wey Hey, man, what have we got here? You three aren't meant to be in here, you know. You will get me the sack. Hang on there whilst I turn on some more lights and take a closer look at you."

"What a funny accent he has," said Charlie not realising that his voice would echo around the room. Fred told Charlie to keep his voice down. With all the lights now turned on, it was very obvious that the hairy dog was in fact an Afghan Hound and, wearing the clothes that he did, Fred thought that he looked like an old hippie. As the dog approached Fred, Charlie and Belvedere for a second time, Charlie seemed unsure and stood back so Fred would have to deal with the dog first.

"Well, well, well, three holes in the ground, what do we have here, two ravens and a Gronkiedoddle! I met one of your lot years ago, but no one would believe that I had met a Gronk, so I stopped telling everyone. Now, what can I do for you?"

Fred stepped forward and explained all about the quest they had been set and how The Great Gob would crown the Grand Masters should they complete the challenge. He then produced the CD and told the hairy dog that they were looking for somewhere to play it. The hairy dog took off his dark sunglasses and polished them with the end of his shirt before speaking.

"I have heard that there was a quest on, set by The Great Gob himself. Oh, forgive my rudeness. I am Roadie, the caretaker here at Rock Circus, the finest display of musical talent in the world."

"You speak funny," suddenly blurted Charlie without warning. Fred kicked Charlie as hard as he could on his shin, hoping that he might keep his beak shut for once. Little chance of that, thought Belvedere, as he glared at Charlie.

"Yeah, man, you are right. I do. I have lived in London for many years, but I originally came from Newcastle. I used to work for some of the great bands like the Rolling Bones and Dimple Kinds. Ahhh, there are too many to mention, but then I got the job here. Anyway to answer your question, I do have a CD player, but there is a problem!"

Fred, Charlie and Belvedere looked at each other. A Problem! They could not have a problem. Time was getting short.

Roadie explained, "You see, man, the problem is, I can play the CD, but I have no idea where it would be heard, so we will have to go through the whole of Rock Circus with the special head phones on as all the music and CD's are controlled by infra red. Let me explain. As you walk up to a model of an artist, then the music of that the artist sings and when you walk away, it stops. If I put your CD on, I have no idea who, what or where it will be played."

Fred and Charlie did not mind going through the whole attraction to see where the clue was, but, as they explained to Roadie, time was getting short. Soon the morning sun would rise and then, if they had not found the clue, they would have to hide somewhere and return the next night. Roadie agreed and quickly found some headphones that would fit them, including a special pair for Belvedere.

Roadie slipped off and placed the CD into the player whilst Fred, Charlie and Belvedere got used to their headphones. On his return they were ready for their tour and hopeful of finding their next clue.

Mustafat, Saber and Foil were, however, were still being bored by Flavel's stories. At one point Mustafat had fallen asleep, only to be woken again by Flavel slapping him on his legs to attract his attention.

Back at the Tower Ripper was still trying to find out what had happened to Fred and Charlie and had taken Sweeney and Todd to the top of Tower Bridge for a chat. Sweeney and Todd had explained that a cat called Mustafat had nearly caught Fred, Charlie and Belvedere. Ripper thought for a while, then, with a click of his wing, he had it!

"Now, listen, you two, I want you to go to Kensington Gardens at first light and ask Lucif's bodyguards if they have heard anything. But be careful, be natural, and be discreet. I don't want Lucif after Fred and Charlie as well. Try and find out if this Mustafat is working for Lucif. I have heard his name before, but know very little about him. When you have found out this information come back and tell me."

Ripper suddenly became all of a fluster. He had spotted Sledger on one of the Tower roofs and, if he was looking for him and could not find him, he would report back to Hector and it would mean more trouble. With a pat on the back Ripper left Sweeney and Todd to follow his orders.

As Sweeney and Todd watched Ripper fly back to the Tower they rested a wing on each other's shoulder.

"That Ripper is a bit of a coward really. I am sure he is

frightened of Hector, same as Eugene was before they sent him off to Wales," said Sweeney laughing, as Ripper once again began to scrub the Tower's roofs.

"I agree, Sweeney, but he has got some brains. I mean, if he becomes Grand Master, well we will be in the big time and no one will mess with us," said Todd unsure why Sweeney was questioning Ripper's authority and making fun of him.

Meanwhile Fred, Charlie and Belvedere were having a wonderful time. Roadie explained how Stevie Wonder had visited Rock Circus and how Bob Geldof had arranged a worldwide concert in 1985 for the starving children in Ethiopia which raised millions of pounds. Charlie, who had seen Michael Jackson, tried to copy his famous moonwalk, but it did not look as good as when Michael did it. Onward they went through Rock Circus, but still they had not heard the clue.

Mustafat, who was now sound asleep, had no idea how bored Saber and Foil were. Flavel was going on about his experience at the battle of Nag's Crossing and all they could do was to nod in the right places, knowing that in a short while morning would break and they had no excuse to remain in the company of Flavel.

Roadie, who now sat in the café at Rock Circus, could not understand why they had not heard the clue, but he reassured Fred, Charlie and Belvedere that they still had one more part to see and the clue had to be in that part of the attraction. Fred let out a sigh. Charlie was unsure if it was a sigh of relief or concern. Roadie, who had left them at the table, opened a large set of doors and told them to follow him. Gathering the satchel together and making sure Belvedere was all right, they followed Roadie into yet another room.

The room had a large stage in it that was hidden by large black curtains that had been drawn. In front of the stage seats swept round in a half moon shape. There were enough seats for at least a hundred, if not more. No sooner had Fred, Charlie and Belvedere sat down than hundreds of animals rushed in from another door. Roadie explained that at this time in the early hours of the morning he always tested this part of the attraction and every night hundreds would come from far and wide to watch. As the room filled, coughs, mutters and whispers came from the lips of the new arrivals. Charlie, who loved attention, felt very important as many of the animals stared at him, Fred and Belvedere. Finally Roadie stood before all the seated animals and whistled so silence would fall.

"Thank you, thank you, thank you. We have an extra surprise for you all tonight. I would like to present to you Fred, Charlie and Belvedere the future Grand Masters of London."

A huge applause could be heard as all the animals cheered and clapped. Charlie immediately got to his feet and took a bow, much to the embarrassment of Fred and Belvedere. Roadie, not wanting Charlie to hold the proceedings up, continued as Fred pulled Charlie down into his seat.

"Now then, time is short, so I will hurry. I hope you will enjoy the show and please come again."

As Roadie took his seat next to Charlie, the lights began to dim. Fred could feel Charlie take hold of his wing and grip it tightly. Then the brilliance of the show began. The lights and the sounds were fantastic. Wax models performed their favourite songs of years gone by. The history of Rock and Roll was played to the animals whilst they sat on the edge of their seats, tapping their paws or claws. At one point Fred thought he had heard the beginning of the clue but it had been Phil Collins singing 'In The Air Tonight'.

Bruce Springsteen, The Beatles, and the Eurythmics all played. The show was just brilliant. But it was not to last.

Just as the music reached an all time high the doors at the end of the room burst open making everyone jump. Bright light flooded the dark room from the corridor outside.

"Hey, man, what is going on?" shouted Roadie, leaping to his feet. It was the fastest Fred and Charlie had seen him move all night. The silhouetted figure in the doorway was dressed in the strangest way. He was wearing a flying jacket with a very large furry collar, baggy trousers and the silliest hat anyone had ever seen. Slowly the strange figure stepped forward.

"Wing Commander Bantam Cocksure is the name. Sorry to disturb you and all of that, but I have very important message for Fred, Charlie and Belvedere. You see, I run the courier business out at RAF Hendon Museum, got to keep us pensioners busy, you know. I call it Bantam Transinternational and, seeing the importance of this message, I thought I would deliver it myself."

Fred, Charlie and Belvedere got to their feet. Well, Belvedere actually stood on his seat so he could be seen. Roadie, impatient to hear the message, told the Bantam to get on with it.

"Ah, well, you see, I am not sure I can do that. I have to keep the code of secrecy, you know. It might be that this message is for Fred, Charlie and Belvedere, but never in the history of Bantams has so much responsibility been put on one Bantam....."but Charlie had heard enough of the babbling Bantam.

"Oh, shut up, and get on with it, you Bantam, or tatty old chicken, whatever you are."

Everyone burst into laughter at Charlie's comment. Wing Commander Bantam Cocksure, however, was not so happy, letting his monocle fall from his left eye as a mark of concern. Muttering under his breath, he fumbled through the many pockets he had, obviously trying to find the message.

"No respect for their elders, these young tail snappers. In the old days everyone would have stood up when I entered the room. Can't even recognise an officer when they see one," muttered the Wing Commander. Finally he found what he had been looking for and from deep inside one of his pockets produced a crumpled piece of paper. Smoothing the piece of paper out, the old Bantam began to read aloud,

Dear Fred, Charlie and Belvedere
Sorry about the mix up with the clue, but after
all the confusion with Mustafat I gave you a blank CD.
Here is the clue you need. Mustafat is on your
trail, so take great care.

Sign-Note

Clearing his throat once again the Wing Commander read the clue.

FROM AN ENTERTAINING WALL OF SOUND
A PALATIAL VENUE MUST BE FOUND
OVER HYDE PARK AND JUST BEYOND
THE PALACE YOU SEEK IS BEHIND THE POND

Wing Commander Bantam Cocksure handed the clue to Fred and winked at Belvedere as he twiddled his moustache. Once again the room filled with mutters and whispers as all the other animals wondered what the clue could mean, but before anyone could say any more keys were heard opening one of the doors. It was the human cleaning staff and everyone had to leave.

The rush of the animals making their escape knocked the poor old Wing Commander clean off his feet. Roadie quickly showed Fred, Charlie and Belvedere a quick escape through a secret hatch at the side of the stage. Through a series of passages they followed Roadie going as fast as they could, until finally they came to a window that Roadie opened with ease.

"You will be safe now. Go and solve your clue and get the title of Grand Masters. I have to go now and I am so glad we met."

Charlie hurriedly placed Belvedere into the satchel with the clue and he and his brother hopped out of the window onto a ledge outside. Thanking Roadie, they prepared for flight. Roadie shut the window behind them and was gone.

Mustafat, Saber and Foil, who had managed to get away from Flavel, now stood on a corner of Piccadilly once again, just below where Fred, and Charlie were standing. The two brothers decided that they had to find a safe place to hide and solve the clue. The rain had stopped at last and the sun was peeking over the buildings. They had to move now before anyone saw them.

Taking to the air, Fred and Charlie circled the statue of Eros, a landmark of Piccadilly, before heading up Regent Street. As Mustafat looked up to the sky, he noticed Fred and Charlie, but there was no way he was going to catch them now. Annoyed, Mustafat scratched his claws down a shop window making Saber and Foil shiver. If only they had left Flavel's earlier. That pesky fox, with his boring stories, thought Mustafat. Watching Fred and Charlie disappear, Mustafat shouted at the top of his voice.

"I'll get you, don't think you have escaped. I am with Lucif now." But Fred and Charlie were gone. Mustafat turned to Saber and Foil. "Let's go and meet Lucif."

8
chapter

Kensington bound

As the early morning sun began to rise over the Tower walls, Hector had thought of nothing else but how Fred, Charlie and Belvedere were doing. He knew the quest for The Great London Adventure was a very hard challenge and many dangers lay ahead of them. Gathering up his feathers that had fallen out over the course of the night, Hector sat back down in his office chair, realising how tired he was.

Sledger had put Ripper to work earlier sweeping down the roof of the Bloody Tower and now Ripper could only think of the dirtiest jobs that he could give Sledger once he was Grand Master. Sweeney and Todd were making their way across to Kensington Palace Gardens as Ripper had requested. All the other ravens around the Tower were thinking of the three adventurers, but kept themselves busy by making plans for the big wedding between Janous and Sledger. Even Honourous was crocheting some napkins to keep himself busy.

Bostrum was pacing up and down on the lawns next to the White Tower, with his wings tucked behind his back and his head held low. Everyone sympathised as to how he must be feeling. After all it was his sons that were out on the quest and, like Hector, Bostrum knew the dangers. Borderline, however, was still very busy repairing the damage that Fred and Charlie had caused to his lawns and flowerbeds. He still muttered to himself, but now he was muttering how he wished Fred and Charlie well.

Mustafat, angry that he had lost the chance of capturing Fred and Charlie, was now even more determined to visit Lucif. But before they could go anywhere, they had to cross a very busy road, the main road of Piccadilly. The land of Eastern Promise that was within walking distance would be an ideal place to seek directions, but Saber and Foil knew that to cross the busy road could cost them their lives.

Mustafat decided that there was only one way to cross the road and that was to close their eyes count to three and run. Saber and Foil agreed and Mustafat began the countdown.

"Three, Two, One, GO," shouted Mustafat. With their hearts pounding, Mustafat, Saber and Foil leapt from the safety of the pavement and darted between the onslaught of the traffic. Tyres screeched as cars screamed to a halt. Horns blasted and drivers cursed at them, but to stop would mean certain pain and possible death if they were hit by one of the vehicles. There was no stopping.

Mustafat and Saber reached the other side safely, and both of them let out a sigh of relief. But suddenly there was a loud thud and a whimper from behind them. Foil had not been so lucky.

Saber watched with Mustafat at his side as Foil flew through the air, coming to rest finally in a dustbin at the side of the road only a few feet from where they were standing. A strange silence fell as Foil's ghostly spirit began to rise.

Then the spirit spoke. "One down, eight to go, protect your lives, now on with the show."

With a shower of sparks the ghostly spirit of Foil's body disappeared. Foil's body jerked in the rubbish bin and he sat up with a start.

"What happened? Where am I? Cooorrrrrr, I feel like I have been hit by a train."

Mustafat and Saber could not believe their eyes. They had heard that cats have nine lives, but they had never seen one lose a life. Foil was still rubbing his head as Saber helped him from the rubbish bin. Once Foil had been given a chance to rest and lick himself clean from the smell of stale burgers, it was time for Mustafat, Saber and Foil to move on.

Belvedere had become very uncomfortable since take-off and had promised that at their next resting-place he would find himself a cushion to sit on. In the meantime he hoped that Fred and Charlie would not start any of their flying games like dodging lampposts.

But Fred and Charlie were too tired to think of playing any games. In fact they were so tired that they had been flying around in circles. So once again they headed up Regent Street looking for somewhere to land. With the firm knowledge that they would rest soon, Fred and Charlie mustered their last drop of energy and, as Charlie banked round much to Belvedere's discomfort, Fred shouted across to his brother. "The raven birds are go!"

Charlie flew as fast as he could to keep up with his brother and shouted at the top of his voice much to the delight and concern of the humans below.

"Warp factor five, Fred. We're off to the other side of the frontier."

Fred, who had only just missed some scaffolding poles, banked this way and that followed by Charlie. Belvedere, however, was turning quite green at all the banking, but then he heard the words he had been waiting for.

"Charlie, look, the perfect landing spot."

Without a word Charlie followed Fred to the landing spot, a large open space on a roof amongst all the buildings on Regent Street. With a sudden bump the satchel came to rest as Charlie landed. Yet another successful landing to add to his record, thought Charlie, as he mopped a bead of sweat from his brow. Suddenly daylight burst into the satchel and the little Gronk, dizzy from his flight, stepped out.

"Okay, you two, what on earth do you think you were doing?

How many more times do I have to tell you? Stop messing about when I am in that satchel. You have no idea how sick I feel."

Fred and Charlie hung their heads in shame. They knew that Belvedere was right and they were very sorry. Belvedere, who decided to take a walk and catch his breath, walked over to the edge of the building to see exactly where they were. Looking down the great vast wall below, he noticed that large letters covered the top part of the building.

"H.A.M.L.E.Y.S," the little Gronk read out loud. HAMLEYS, thought Belvedere. That name rang a bell, but what was it? Belvedere paced up and down trying to think, repeatedly saying the word HAMLEYS. Fred, who had heard Belvedere, suddenly got to his feet. "HAMLEYS, the largest toy store in Europe. Oh, WOW, we have landed on the largest toy store, Charlie."

Charlie could not believe his ears. HAMLEYS, a toy store with floor after floor after floor of all the best toys you could ever dream about. Many a time they had passed by the doors and both Fred and Charlie had wished to enter. Looking over at Belvedere, the little Gronk knew what was on their minds.

"OH NO. Come on, chaps. There is no way that we can just walk round the store. It is daylight and we would be certain to be caught by the pest catcher."

Fred and Charlie could not hide their disappointment.

Belvedere thought quickly. He could not see Fred and Charlie sad, but at the same time they had too much to do to go walking around looking at toys. Then, with a snap of his fingers, he had the solution.

"I know what we will do. When we become Grand Masters, we could come back at Christmas and collect all the toys for all the animals that have been born this year and we could make a special delivery to them before Santa delivers their main presents. We could also meet the famous Professor Fingertips Nibulus who is the finest toy maker in the whole of the world. We could even help the Gee Gaws that stack all the shelves at night, so when the Rucksacks (tourists) come the next day all the shelves are full."

Fred and Charlie agreed with Belvedere's plan to return at Christmas, much to his delight, and their sad faces once again turned into smiling happy ones. Sitting down on the roof of HAMLEYS, Fred, Charlie and Belvedere spread out their map of London and began to plan their route for the next stage of the quest.

Mustafat, Saber and Foil had made their way into the heart of the land of Eastern Promise, keeping their eyes open in case they should bump into the boss of the whole of Eastern Promise, Sam Sing. Although Sam Sing was known for keeping Eastern Promise trouble free, everyone in London knew that he was also the finest Chinese cook in the whole of the land and a very good jazz musician. Guarding such a place, full of the best Chinese restaurants in London, had been a hard task as the food was rich pickings for anyone and very often brought unsavoury animals to rummage in the rubbish bins.

Needless to say Mustafat had not asked permission to enter the land of Eastern Promise and Saber and Foil were concerned that they might well be caught and treated as scavengers. So far they had been lucky. No one had seen them. But Mustafat's ear suddenly stood up. He had heard something, much to the concern of Saber and Foil.

Slowly Mustafat edged his way forward, keeping close to the edge of a building that led round a corner. With each step they took Mustafat, Saber and Foil sensed that someone was watching them. Suddenly, behind them, a dust bin lid fell causing quite a noise. Slowly Mustafat, Saber and Foil turned round and were confronted by two large Siamese cats. Not wanting to hang around, they took to their heels followed by the sound of pounding paws behind them. On turning yet another corner, Mustafat came to an abrupt halt. Saber and Foil crashed into the back of him. The three cats now sat in a heap on the floor and in front of them stood Sam Sing and his jazz band.

Sam Sing and the band stopped playing. All eyes fell on Mustafat, Saber and Foil. Concerned that they were now trapped in an alley full of strangers, Mustafat nervously stepped forward.

"Begging your pardon," he said in a squeaky voice. "We seem

to be lost, I was wondering if you could direct us to Kensington Palace. You see we have a meeting with Lucif, The Great Lucif, that is." Mustafat allowed his words to trail off. Surely the name of Lucif would scare the cats that stood before him. Saber and Foil placed their paws over their heads. They could not believe that Mustafat had said to Sam Sing that he was meeting with Lucif. No one ever mentioned meetings with Lucif. It was a rule of the alleys. Slowly Sam Sing put down his shiny trumpet. "As I was saying, if you could just point us in the right direction," stuttered Mustafat. Turning round he noticed that Sam Sing's followers had now blocked all escape routes.

Mustafat summonsed all of his strength and puffed out his chest and fur, trying to make himself bigger and look more mean, at the top of his voice he shouted, "That's it. Don't think that your friends scare me, because they don't. Now let us pass or there will be real trouble."

Saber and Foil could not believe their ears. They were not going to get out of the alley alive if Mustafat continued like this. Without a word Sam Sing stepped forward and removed his straw hat. Brushing the top of it, he spoke quietly. "And what trouble would that be?"

Saber and Foil could see the situation was getting worse and, as they tried to step back, a large ginger cat stopped them and in a mean growl asked if they were going somewhere.

"No. No," replied Saber and Foil. Mustafat could be seen to be shaking from the tip of his tail to his nose but still managed to continue talking as Sam Sing moved closer.

"Errrr, nice weather we are having. Now come on let's not be nasty about all of this. What I meant was, would you like to share this piece of fish with me?"

Mustafat pulled an old smelly fish from his dungaree's and waved it under Sam Sing's nose. The leader of the land of Eastern Promise told Mustafat to put the fish away, holding a paw in front of his nose as the smell was so terrible. Mustafat, not wanting to upset Sam Sing further, tucked the fish back inside his pocket. With the fish safely out of smelling distance, Sam Sing began to question Mustafat.

"So why would the likes of you have a meeting with Lucif? You would not be planning to go after the two ravens and the Gronk would you If you are, that means you are disrupting a very important time for the animals of London. I, for one, would not take too kindly to that."

Sam Sing placed a paw on a very confused Mustafat's shoulder. The silly cat had no idea about a quest or the Great London Adventure. Sam Sing pulled Mustafat closer and whispered in his ear.

"If I hear that you are, Mustafat, I will hand you over to Eager, and he will make you clean every alley in the land of Eastern Promise. And that includes your two little friends there."

Mustafat, Saber and Foil shook their heads and Mustafat gave his word that he was not after the ravens or the Gronk and that the reason for meeting Lucif was simply because he wanted to meet the greatest criminal cat of all time. Sam Sing, who was not totally convinced, allowed Mustafat, Saber and Foil to pass and, as his friends parted forming a gauntlet for them to leave, he patted them on the back making sure they understood the warning he had given them.

As Mustafat, Saber and Foil slowly made their way through the corridor of cats, Sam Sing gave them directions to Kensington Palace and told them where they might find Lucif's bodyguards. Then, just as they were about to turn a corner and scamper off to freedom, Sam Sing's voice echoed through the alley.

"HALT."

The three cats froze to the spot and Mustafat turned to see what Sam Sing wanted.

"If you are ever in the area again, I am playing at Ronnie Botts, the famous cats'jazz club. Just leave the fish at home."

Everyone burst out laughing. Now that they were at a safe distance Mustafat's bravery had returned and he poked his tongue out at Sam Sing before taking to his heels and running as fast as he could. All Saber and Foil could hear as they followed Mustafat was even louder laughter. Neither of them had been laughed at before and they did not like it.

When they were safely away and could not hear the laugher any more, Mustafat stopped for a rest. Leaning against a wall, he puffed and panted. Saber and Foil, however, who were a lot younger, were not out of breath, but very concerned at the promises their boss had made to Sam Sing. And what was The Great London Adventure all about?

Fred, Charlie and Belvedere felt quite rested now. They had eaten some food and cleaned themselves up a bit, and they had even worked out their route to Kensington Palace. Now the three of them had to prepare for the flight. On the roof Belvedere had found an old scarf that he had made into a sort of a cushion, so at least now he would be comfortable in flight. With the firm promise that Fred and Charlie would not bank too hard to the right or left, Belvedere climbed into the satchel and once again they took to the skies.

Mustafat and his two, now uncertain helpers were on the way to Kensington Palace, this time taking great care of the roads, especially Foil. Little did they know that Fred, Charlie and Belvedere were heading to the same destination from a different part of London.

The preparations back at the Tower for the wedding were going very well indeed. Borderline had made wonderful flower decorations whilst the other ravens were busy polishing railings and sweeping steps. Sander, one of the best raveness carpenters, was building the stage where Fred, Charlie and Belvedere were going to be crowned and where Janous and Sledger would be married. Bristle and Turps had even started painting some of the walls and benches so that the place would look as good as new when the two big ceremonies took place. The Tower was beginning to look very grand and regal. Sledger had now positioned Ripper on the roof of Byward Tower so he could signal if the Raven Master (a Human) should leave his house. But as always Ripper did not have his mind on the job, for Sweeney and Todd had returned from visiting the bodyguards of Lucif.

"Did you see them, what happened, tell me?" questioned Ripper. Sweeney and Todd were still trying to get their breath. It had been a long and hard flight. Sweeney raised his wing as Ripper once again questioned what had happened. Ripper, who was impatient to hear the news, rolled his eyes and tutted under his breath. Finally Sweeney spoke, but still panting.

"Well, I'll tell you. You have never in your life seen cats this big. We are talking huge. We took a great risk in just landing, let alone talking to them." Ripper impatiently banged his beak together ordering Sweeney to continue. "Well, Ripper, I don't know how you think you are going to be Grand Master and capture the book of The Great London Adventure! First of all, Lucif's guards tell me that they have heard that Mustafat is after Fred, Charlie and Belvedere. The stupid cat just wants to catch them and has no idea about The Great London Adventure or its significance. Second of all, Lucif does know about the quest and wants the book and title for himself, but cannot be seen to be going after it himself. So what he has up his sleeve no one knows! Also, what you have to take into consideration, Ripper, is that many of the animals around London are in fact helping Fred, Charlie and Belvedere. So how do you think that you are going to capture the book and become Grand Master?"

Ripper was astonished that Sweeney and Todd should question him in such a way. Ripper sat down banging his beak together as he always did when he was angry. Deep in thought the evil raven began to plan. Sweeney and Todd waited patiently for him to come up with his master plan, if, that is, he could!

Suddenly an evil look spread across Rippers face as he looked up at Sweeney, and then Todd.

"You leave the problems of getting my title of Grand Master to me. There is only one place that I can steal the book from and that is from right here in the Tower when The Great Gob brings it to present to Fred, Charlie and the Gronk. It is then that I shall steal it and demand my title."

Sweeney and Todd looked at Ripper. They thought it could work, but would he get away with it? Unsure, but willing to go along with the plan, Sweeney and Todd shook Ripper's wing. He then suggested that they return to Kensington Gardens and see if Fred, Charlie and Belvedere turned up. Reluctantly Sweeney and Todd headed off, leaving Ripper to pace up and down his roof.

Fred and Charlie were making good time. They had left

HAMLEYS behind them and kept their flying as straight as possible for Belvedere's sake. Before long they would be in the grounds of Kensington Palace and on their way to solving the next clue. Below them Fred and Charlie noticed a vast park.

"That has to be it, Charlie, look. In the distance there is a round pond and beyond that a large building, set in fine grounds, that has to be the Palace."

Fred and Charlie increased their speed and although there was a slight head wind, the two brothers were flying quite fast.

"Mustafat can't touch us now," shouted Fred. Charlie simply nodded in agreement. He was more interested in flying straight and not upsetting Belvedere. The little Gronk, who was pleased that the ride this time was pleasant, decided that he would take a look out of his little hole. To his amazement they were flying very close to the ground and as they started to bank round gently Belvedere suddenly realised why. Charlie was circling a pond and the Gronkiedoddle grew concerned that he might begin to fly dangerously.

"WOW! Fred, look at that. It is a large pond."

"Yes, I know, Charlie, but come on, we don't have any time for sightseeing or playing in the pond."

Charlie agreed and once again Fred and Charlie began flying in the direction of Kensington Palace.

Mustafat, Saber and Foil managed to escape the alleyways of the land of Eastern Promise and had made their way to Green Park tube (underground) station. They were fascinated by all the expensive cars that had pulled up outside The Ritz Hotel just along from where they were standing. Mustafat, being Mustafat, had considered nipping round the back of the hotel and going through the rubbish bins for some food, but had thought better of it. Then to Saber and Foil's amazement, Mustafat had an idea.

"Look at all these cars. One of them will surely be going past Kensington Gardens or even the Palace. If we listen out, we could jump on the back bumper and hitch a ride. It would save our paws and get us there a lot quicker."

Saber thought it was a brilliant idea, but Foil was not so sure. He had grown to dislike cars and was worried that he may fall and lose another life. Mustafat and Saber promised that they would help him and so, reluctantly, he agreed. The three cats did not have to wait long before they heard a very well dressed woman ask for her limousine to take her to Kensington Palace for the garden party. As the limousine pulled away Mustafat, Saber and Foil jumped on the back bumper.

Once safely on, the three cats sat back to enjoy their ride. Cars hooted and buses flashed their lights, but the driver of the limousine took no notice. Past Hyde Park Barracks they drove and on to Rutland gate. Mustafat knew exactly where they were as his home, the Royal Albert Hall, was just up the road. Oh, how he wished that someone he knew would see him riding on the back of the limousine, but as they sped past his home no one was around. Then, as the limousine turned right, they were inside the Palace grounds.

Fred and Charlie had only just landed in the grounds to Kensington Palace and had no idea Mustafat was so close. Belvedere climbed out of the satchel and praised Fred and Charlie on such a wonderful landing. He thought that if he told them each time they landed well how good they were, it would build their confidence, and eventually they would land perfectly each time. So far his plan seemed to be working.

Fred and Charlie looked about whilst Belvedere read the clue once again. Then, as Fred was about to take a sniff of the flowers, a face appeared and he took a deep sniff of fur. Charlie looked at his brother as his beak curled and a large sneeze blew many of the petals of the flowers to the ground. Standing back Fred was confronted by the face of a very very beautiful rabbit. The rabbit stepped out from the bush and introduced herself.

"Hello, my name is Petula, and I am the groundkeeper's daughter. You must leave this place. You are in great danger."

Petula looked about, obviously looking to see that no one was watching them. Fred and Charlie were very confused. Had Belvedere read the map correctly? Perhaps they were in the wrong place! Belvedere walked forward and greeted the rabbit, who kissed him gently on his forehead. Charlie was jealous. He wanted a kiss, but Belvedere was explaining who they were and why they had come.

"Oh I know who you are, and why you are here, but Lucif lives very close and his bodyguards are out looking for you right now. I have also heard that a cat by the name of Mustafat has arrived on the back of a limousine."

Fred and Charlie took a deep breath at the mention of Mustafat's name confirming to them that he was obviously working with Lucif. Belvedere sat down on the grass and pondered what they should do, but it was Petula that came up with the plan.

"You must leave here, and go and see the Chief Justice Filo Mackay. He lives on the road called The Strand in a building called The Royal Courts Of Justice. He is the judge for all the animals. It is the only chance you have to complete the quest. He will issue you with a new clue. Now, please go, before they catch you."

Charlie's heart sank at the prospect of having to fly once again before he had rested, but being captured by Mustafat or, even worse Lucif, was not an option. Just then there was a loud rustle from the bushes behind them. Belvedere quickly slipped into the satchel hoping that whatever or whoever had made the noise had not seen him. Petula pushed Fred and Charlie out of the way.

"Go, I will tell whoever it is that you have left. Go to Filo. He will tell you what to do. and send him my love."

Fred and Charlie took to the air. The satchel was still open and, as Belvedere clung on for his life, the bushes parted and two very large cats stepped out. Fred and Charlie knew that there was nothing they could do for Petula and as they climbed higher into the sky they watched as Petula was led off into the bushes. Fred and Charlie hoped that she was all right and no harm would come to her. Belvedere, concerned that he still might fall, shouted for Charlie to land, but Charlie managed to fly one winged and safely secured the satchel buckle. Now Belvedere was at least safe as they continued their flight to find Chief Justice Filo.

Belvedere quickly studied the map inside the cramped satchel and shouted out the directions so Fred and Charlie did not get lost.

"Back track on yourselves and use the landmarks we passed to get here to go back to HAMLEYS. Once there, carry on down Regent Street, turn left at Piccadilly Circus, then fly over Nelson's Column, then just past Charing Cross train station and fly straight down The Strand."

Charlie and Fred shouted to let Belvedere know that they had heard the directions and thanked him. They were really working as a team.

Mustafat, Saber and Foil leapt from the limousine and took cover in the bushes, only moments after Fred and Charlie had taken to the air and Lucif's bodyguards had captured Petula. Mustafat would have been so angry if he had known that he had just missed Fred and Charlie, but his meeting with Lucif meant that he could think of nothing else.

Crouched in the bushes Mustafat, Saber and Foil waited for some passing humans to go into the Palace. Saber, still worried, decided that this was the only chance he might get to talk some sense into Mustafat. Quietly he whispered to Mustafat. "Why don't we go home and forget all about meeting Lucif? We can put our feet up and avoid any problems with Sam Sing and his gang and go back to living a normal life."

"Sounds like a good idea to me."

Mustafat turned to Foil, and snarled at him. One mutineer in the ranks was bad enough but two, Mustafat could not have that. Foil looked at Mustafat with a puzzled and concerned look on his face.

"I didn't say anything."

Mustafat laughed out loud, surprised that Foil was trying to deny his outburst, and told Saber that they were not going home.

"Like I said, I think you should go home," came the voice again, but this time Mustafat knew that it was not Saber or Foil, as their lips never moved. Mustafat's fur shot up on end.

Turning round, Mustafat looked up at a very large well-built cat. The cat leaned forward and placed his nose against Mustafat's, who was now shaking from head to paw.

"So what are you doing here?"

Mustafat stood back as the large cat ran a paw across his head and began to look Saber and Foil up and down.

"Errrrr, we have come to meet with Lucif. I have some very important news for him," said Mustafat, trying very hard not to look scared.

"The name is Omph, and you have to tell me what you want with Lucif, as I am his Bodyguard. Got it?" snapped Omph, enjoying seeing Mustafat, Saber and Foil quiver at his words.

Mustafat cleared his throat and looked up at Omph hoping that his voice would not squeak with fear. "Flavel told us to come with our news. He told us that we could see Lucif. You see I have a deal for him regarding two ravens."

"Flavel eh? Well, you had better come with me, but if you are wasting Lucif's time you will be in deep trouble, or worse," snarled Omph before turning and hurrying through the bushes. Mustafat set off as quickly as he could go, with Saber and Foil following behind. They really hoped that Mustafat knew what he was doing and had remembered not to mention the missing claw on Lucif's front paw. As they travelled through the undergrowth Mustafat thought that Omph looked very mean in his black combats and black jumper, and the baseball cap turned round on his head, looked especially good. He would have to get himself an outfit like that if he were to become part of Lucif's gang, instead of his old dungarees.

Prickly thorns and broken branches hindered their route, but still Mustafat, Saber and Foil kept up. Then, without warning, they entered a clearing, surrounded by high bushes. Standing by what looked like a doorway at the bottom of a large oak tree stood two more very large cats dressed in the same clothes as Omph. By their sides Mustafat noticed that they had skate boards.

Omph told Mustafat to wait where he was and wandered over to his friends. For a while they chatted and Mustafat wished he could hear what they were saying. He also wished he could have a go on their skateboards, but thought he had better not ask for a go. Omph then whistled for Mustafat, Saber and Foil to join them.

"This is it, boys, the big time, a meeting with the master criminal himself."

Slowly Mustafat walked over to Omph and he introduced Fisticuff and Heckle, his two friends. Mustafat held out a paw, but they chose to ignore it. Then another large cat appeared at the door in the oak tree and told Omph to send the prisoners down. Prisoners, thought Mustafat, as he entered the entrance that led into a corridor that was littered with old fish bones and cat food tin lids.

"I knew it," muttered Saber, as he was pushed into the corridor followed by Foil. They had walked into a trap and Mustafat still could not see it. At the end of the corridor was another door and the large cat knocked on it. From inside came a loud, scary 'YES' and, as the door opened, Mustafat, Saber and Foil were pushed in.

Once inside Mustafat, Saber and Foil stood in a huge room. At the end of the room sat Lucif in a large chair that looked like a throne. A long table was covered in food and guards lined the walls. There was no escape for Mustafat or Saber and Foil.

"AH HA, Mustafat, the cat that wants to be me, and his very small bodyguards. Come closer, Mustafat, and let me smell the fear and see the panic in your eyes."

Mustafat did as he was told, but Lucif did not need to look into his eyes or smell his fear, because Saber and Foil could hear his teeth chattering with fright. And if they could, so could Lucif. As Mustafat moved closer to Lucif, he began to explain how he wanted to capture Fred and Charlie and that he had no need for the Gronk. Lucif listened and then removed a dart from his top pocket and threw it at Mustafat, the dart flew through the air and missed his head by a fraction before it stuck in the far wall. Mustafat was left standing, unable to talk, with a very large parting in his fur on the top of his head. Saber and Foil could not believe their eyes. Lucif rose to his feet and pointed at Mustafat.

"So why should I help you capture these ravens? You should be helping me. I am the Master Genius Criminal of all time. I am the one that all live in fear of and I am the one who is now bored of you. Kill them," ordered Lucif to Mustafat's horror.

In desperation Mustafat shouted out whilst Saber and Foil clung to each other. "Wait, Lucif, I beg you. You cannot be seen to capture these ravens, not that I should think you would want to. I simply offered the Gronk to do with as you see fit, he is no use, I know. I tell you what I will do. You can have one of the ravens. But the advantage of me going after them, with some help from your bodyguards if I should need it, would be, should you get caught capturing the ravens then the Great Gob would send you away forever and you would lose all your power. Where as, if I get caught, then I can plead ignorance as a petty criminal and he would let me off. But if I do get them, then you have a raven and a Gronk for nothing."

Lucif smiled. Mustafat was even more stupid than he thought and he had no idea about the quest and the value of the ravens or even the Gronk. Lucif rubbed his paws together. Mustafat was in his evil grasp and was going to carry out his dirty work.

"Very well, you can capture the ravens and use my bodyguards if you need them, but remember you work for me now. And should you fail with this capture, well, I don't think I need to say any more."

Mustafat leapt into the air. He had achieved his dream, working for Lucif. Saber and Foil were now very concerned. Mustafat might have his dream, but if they did not capture the ravens, then they dreaded what might happen. And their track record of getting close to capturing the ravens had not been good. Then, as Mustafat turned and winked at Saber and Foil, one of Lucif's bodyguards whispered in his ear. Lucif raised his paw and Mustafat stood to attention.

"I have just heard that these ravens you talk about are on their way to the Royal Courts of Justice. Somewhere I know very well. It is there that you must catch them and bring them to me. I shall decide which raven I shall have and the Gronkiedoddle is mine. Now go, and don't fail." With that Lucif turned his back on Mustafat. One of the bodyguards then blindfolded Mustafat, Saber and Foil and led them from the room through a different door. Not worried at all because he was now one of Lucif's elite gang, Mustafat followed the bodyguard hanging onto his belt. Saber and Foil, who were both clinging to Mustafat, followed without saying a word. It was then that Mustafat noticed the strong smell of rubbish and sewage. They were in the sewer pipes that ran under the whole of London. So that was how Lucif moved about so quickly and could disappear if there was any trouble.

Nearly at the Royal Courts Of Justice, Fred and Charlie were looking forward to landing and feeling the ground under their clawed feet. With the edge of the building inches from their claws, Fred and Charlie touched down. Their wings ached and beads of sweat fell from their beaks. They had made it. If only they knew that Mustafat was close by and on his way to capture them!

9
chapter
The Royal Courts

Tired, Fred and Charlie rested on the roof of the Royal Courts Of Justice whilst Belvedere organised some food. With all the flying the two brothers had to keep their strength up.

Mustafat, Saber and Foil were still being led blindfolded through the sewers under London. The smell that had become worse seemed not to bother them any more. They would just be happy to see daylight. The bodyguard that was escorting them had not spoken a word. Silently he marched on, taking a turn to the left or to the right. Mustafat, Saber and Foil would never find their way back to Lucif's secret hideout, that was for certain.

Sweeney and Todd, who had just landed at Kensington Palace, had found a feather belonging to either Fred or Charlie and a tuft of rabbit fur. Heckle, who had chatted with the two curious birds earlier, was wondering why they had returned and, as he approached Sweeney and Todd, he sensed that they were looking for something.

"So what are you two doing back so soon?"questioned Heckle, making Sweeney and Todd nearly jump out of their feathers.

"Oh, well, you know, we liked the place so much we thought that we would drop by again,"said Sweeney, trying to be as cool as he could. Heckle, however, was not convinced and decided to take the two visitors to Lucif. Sweeney and Todd knew that they had no choice, but to follow Heckle. A forceful invite, Sweeney thought. Lucif, who was still sitting in his throne room, could not believe how popular he was today.

"More visitors. My, my, now what have these two been up to, or should I say wanting?"

Lucif, who had been relaxing reading his paper when his two uninvited guests had arrived, screwed his paper up and threw it in the corner.

"No, no, sir, er, Lucif, er, Boss. Er, we just called into the gardens up above to have another look around, very beautiful up there,"said Sweeney, trying to act as innocent as possible.

"Don't lie to me,"shouted Lucif, fluffing up all his fur and knocking a cup of milk to the floor. Sweeney and Todd knew that they had been caught and obviously Lucif knew why they had come. In fear of their lives Sweeney and Todd stood looking at the floor, not knowing what to say. Lucif rose to his feet and banged his paw down on the corner of the throne.

"I know who you are, and that you are friends of that Ripper. I bet he has sent you here to get hold of the book The Great London Adventure and the title that goes with it. Well, he can't have it, it is mine, all mine."

Lucif laughed so loudly that the cups on the table began to shake. Sweeney and Todd had never seen anything like it before. Suddenly Lucif stopped laughing and turned on Sweeney and Todd. Lucif's eyes seemed to glow red with evil.

"Now you go back to Ripper and tell him from me, if I hear that he has even touched a feather of Fred and Charlie and a hair of that Gronkiedoddle he will have me to answer, to."

Sweeney and Todd agreed that they would carry out Lucif's request and deliver the message to Ripper. Two of Lucif's bodyguards took hold of Sweeney and Todd and led them from the room as Lucif ordered another paper.

Once outside, the two bodyguards warned Sweeney and Todd that Lucif was very serious and to pass the message on. Sweeney and Todd had every intention of telling Ripper. In fact they were going back to the London Dungeon, never to leave again. Without a further word they took off, faster than they had ever flown before.

A strange light made Mustafat, Saber and Foil blink several times before they could see properly as their blindfolds were removed. Still underground, in a corridor lit only by candles, they were told to knock on the steel door in front of them and one of Lucif's retired kerb thieves would answer. The bodyguard that had escorted them all the way then vanished, leaving the three of them alone.

Saber and Foil sighed with relief that they had not come to

a sticky end and still had their fur intact, but Saber was not happy.

"Well done, Mustafat, we now work for Lucif, who by the way is not going to let us get away with this. Do you really think that he is going to let us keep one of the ravens? You saw his bodyguards."

But Mustafat was not listening and pounded his paw on the steel door.

As Mustafat waited for a reply, Fred, Charlie and Belvedere sat on the roof above.

"Found a way in yet, Belvedere?"asked Fred after a sandwich of peanut butter, worms and stale raisins. Taking a few minutes to reply, the little Gronk suddenly shouted, 'I've got it' and described a route that he thought was the safest to get into the courts. To their right was a roof hatch that Belvedere had found and it was open, but he was too small to lift it on his own. If they were careful they could gain access to the building this way, but Belvedere did not have a plan of the inside of the building, so they would have to find their way around once inside. Charlie lifted the hatch and, to their surprise, there was steps leading down.

Inside, the building smelt old and the marble floor seemed cold on their feet. Expensive paintings lined the walls, and on one wall there was a large mosaic. On the floor a plaque read 'Designed by Mr Street in 1882'. Belvedere suddenly remembered that he had visited the courts some time ago and could just about remember his way around. Then, from a large door, a rabbit dressed in very fine robes appeared. It was Chief Justice Filo Mackay.

Looking up, the rabbit noticed the little Gronk and then Fred and Charlie. He seemed happy to see them and, as he approached them, he offered a warm hello. Belvedere explained that they had been sent to him because of the trouble they had experienced with Mustafat and Lucif, and that because of them they had to look for another clue to continue the quest. When Belvedere explained to Chief Justice Filo Mackay that Petula had been captured as they escaped, he sat down in a near by chair with a bump. Fred and Charlie, seeing that he was obviously upset, placed a wing round him.

"Petula, captured. Oh my, Lucif. Oh my."

Chief Justice Filo Mackay hung his head, shaking it from side to side. The meanest cat in the whole of London had captured his long lost sweetheart. Fred and Charlie had no idea what to do and Belvedere stood at Filo's feet patting them, saying that he was sure she would be all right. Suddenly Filo rose to his feet.

"Right, we have work to do. We have to stop Lucif once and for all and you two have to continue with the quest. I shall deal with Lucif and get Petula out of his clutches. I have clues in my office safe especially for this type of situation and with you safely on your way I can sort Lucif out,"explained Filo, with a real sense of determination in his voice. Wasting no time, Chief Justice Filo Mackay told Fred, Charlie and Belvedere to follow him to his office.

Deep down below the street outside the Royal Courts of Justice Mustafat, Saber and Foil, who now were very smelly and wet through, heard as someone began to unbolt the large metal door. Slowly the door began to open and then stopped. Mustafat pushed Saber and Foil through first. To their surprise they found themselves in a disused toilet. Suddenly a voice spoke from the shadows.

"I have been expecting you. We have work to do."

Looking about, Mustafat, Saber and Foil noticed that a ferret dressed in a long coat, big boots and a large floppy hat was standing in the corner with his arms crossed.

"Anklesnap is the name. Lucif phoned me to let me know you would be arriving. The ravens and the Gronk you are after have arrived. I heard them talking to Chief Justice Filo Mackay up there."

Anklesnap pointed to the ceiling with a scowl on his face. Mustafat, Saber and Foil got the impression that he did not like Filo Mackay or upstairs. As the ferret walked closer to Mustafat, Saber and Foil, they noticed that his fur was oily and dirty and that his clothes looked like they had not been washed in years. As Anklesnap removed his hat and banged it against his coat a cloud of dust rose, causing Mustafat to cough.

"Enough of that coughing. You must get up those stairs and into the main building,"snapped the ferret pointing to a very old set of steps that disappeared into the roof of the disused toilet. Mustafat, Saber and Foil looked up the steps and did not like the look of them. They looked very old and unsafe. They knew they had no choice but to climb them, but before they did, Anklesnap offered a word of advice.

"Watch out for that Filo Mackay. If he catches you, he will make sure that you spend the next thirty years down here with me."

The three cats looked at each other without saying a word. The closer they got to capturing Fred and Charlie and hopefully the Gronk as well, the more risks they were taking, and even Mustafat was beginning to wonder if it was all worth it. Without even a goodbye to Anklesnap, Mustafat, Saber and Foil began to climb the steps and all they could hear as they climbed higher and higher was the evil laugh of the dirty ferret who lived in the toilet.

As the trap door in the broom cupboard opened, Foil was the first to climb out, followed by Saber and then Mustafat. The light that was coming from under the door gave them just enough light to see what they were doing. On the count of three Foil opened the door and ran out into the main building. Saber, who would not leave his friend on his own, followed, but Mustafat would only come out once they had told him no one was about.

Not a noise could be heard apart from the distant snoring of a human who had to be the guard. Mustafat looked about whilst Saber and Foil placed a large vase in front of the broom cupboard door, ensuring that it did not close and leave them without an escape route.

In the distance Mustafat could hear voices as he approached a large staircase. It had to be Fred and Charlie, he thought, as he beckoned the other two to join him. Saber then noticed a raven feather on the floor. Mustafat was right. They were close to Fred and Charlie! Quietly the three of them crept up the staircase and with each step the voices became louder.

Inside Filo's office files were piled high and old cups of tea littered the floor. The desk where Filo was now sitting could hardly be seen with all the paper work that was piled high all over it. In the middle of the mess Filo was scribbling on a piece of paper. He was writing down everything that Belvedere, Fred and Charlie had told him about Mustafat, Lucif, what had happened at the Royal Albert Hall, and even how helpful Roadie had been. At last Filo Mackay put his pen down.

"Now then, we seem to have a problem with Mustafat. I have come across him before, which is why I sent him to the Royal Albert Hall to work, I was hoping that the music might settle him down a bit, but obviously it has not. The main worry is that he has teamed up with Lucif. Now that I can't understand unless Lucif is using him to get to you. Mustafat is not the most intelligent of cats and I could see how Lucif could lead him along, letting him think that he was working for him. But then, when he has served his purpose, well, who knows what he might do."

Mustafat, who was now listening at the door of Filo's office, could not believe his ears. What did he know. He was the Chief of Justice and knew nothing of Lucif. Saber and Foil looked at Mustafat They knew that Filo was talking sense, but still Mustafat could not see it and, as Filo continued, Mustafat became more and more outraged.

"You see, I know Lucif so very well. I was the one that sent him to Trickston Nick for life, that's a large prison on the other side of London. But he escaped and I have to say a very brave escape it was, and then all these animals were getting caught doing things they should not and of course they were brought here. Well, they used to tell me how Lucif had tricked them and led them on saying that he would make them his second in command."

Just then Belvedere heard a noise coming from outside the office door. Placing his thimble of tea down on the desk, Filo got up and walked to the door. On opening it he found that there was no one in sight, but he was certain he could hear the distant murmuring of a cat in pain.

"Belvedere, you wait here. Fred, Charlie, come with me, we are going to investigate, We shall leave this door open and should you see anything, shout."

Belvedere agreed that he would, whilst Fred and Charlie wondered why they had to go and investigate. After all it might be Mustafat and it was them he was after. Without any choice, Fred and Charlie followed Filo Mackay down the stairs, stopping at the bottom. The wise old rabbit took from his robes a large magnifying glass. Fred and Charlie wondered what he was doing, as he bent over and began looking at some mud on the floor.

"Just as I thought. Mustafat's paw prints, and I would say that the other set of prints belong to Saber and Foil. They are here and that is for certain. Mustafat must have become very brave in his old age."

"Belvedere is on his own"shouted Fred and Charlie, but it was too late. Before they had a chance to climb the stairs Mustafat had appeared at the top with the tiny little Gronk gripped in his paw.

"Don't move. Ha, ha, Filo Mackay, how wrong you are. I am not stupid and Lucif would not do that to me. I am too important. Now, if you want to see the little chap again meet me, er, meet me, errrrrr."

Mustafat was lost for words. He had no idea where they could meet him, until, that is, Saber mentioned London Zoo.

"London Zoo in a week."

"In two days,"whispered Saber, explaining to Mustafat that in a week the whole of the animals of London could be trained and ready to recapture the Gronk.

"In two days at London Zoo."

Fred and Charlie felt helpless as Mustafat, Saber and Foil disappeared and, after only a few seconds, the sound of a large trap door slamming shut echoed round the building. Fred and Charlie turned to Chief Justice Mackay.

"Well, what are we to do now? Mustafat has Belvedere and that will mean that he will take him to Lucif,"said Fred, very worried about Belvedere's safety. Charlie had puffed himself up as much as he could and was muttering under his breath. His brother had never seen him so angry. Filo Mackay raised his large rabbit's foot.

"Don't worry, we shall get Belvedere back safely, but Mustafat now has a charge of kidnap hanging over him as do Saber and Foil. Very serious charges. Come on, we have no time to lose."

Filo Mackay rushed back to his office followed by Fred and Charlie. As they arrived at the office, they noticed that all of Filo's files were scattered and the cups of tea had been knocked over. Belvedere had obviously put up a very brave fight. Picking up the phone Filo Mackay spoke to The Great Gob and explained the circumstances and that Belvedere was now in the grip of Mustafat and certainly Lucif. He also mentioned that Lucif had Petula.

For some time The Great Gob talked with Filo and, as he did so, the rabbit scribbled pages of notes. Finally he thanked the great ruler and hung up the phone.

"WELL, what did he say?"asked Fred, agitated that he did not hear what The Great Gob had said. After all it was his idea for them to come on the quest. Filo sat down at his desk and told Fred and Charlie to do the same.

"Right. The Great Gob has said that the three of you have done very well to get this far, and that you have to forget the quest. Belvedere's safe return is more important. Now everyone knows that The Great Gob could defeat Lucif and that would be an end to things, but if he does that, then he will simply return at a later date and start his bad behaviour all over again. No, it is down to you two. That way, when you defeat Lucif, he will be the laughing-stock of the whole of London and word will spread throughout the animal kingdom, the length and breadth of the country, and he will be finished."

Fred and Charlie looked at each other. They could not defeat the great master criminal of London. Charlie, however, was very unhappy that The Great Gob could not help them and began pacing up and down the office. Fred had to chuckle because he looked just like their father when he became upset. Filo, who was looking through one of his filing cabinets, suddenly held a piece of paper in the air.

"I have got it,"shouted Filo and Charlie turned round to see what he was so excited about. Filo now spread a map out on his desk and beckoned Fred and Charlie to take a closer look.

"Now, Stanton, the old war dog, is the best army trainer in the country and he has experience of dealing with situations like this. He is the one that will help you. You have two days to prepare and that should be enough if you hurry."

Filo pointed out on the map where Stanton lived and Fred and Charlie made sure they had the route firmly in their minds, as they would not have time to stop and read maps. Folding the map up, Charlie placed it in the satchel. The satchel seemed so light without the Gronk and would be a constant reminder to Charlie that he was a captive of Mustafat and Lucif. Filo assured Fred and Charlie that when Lucif and Mustafat were captured he would enforce the harshest punishments on them. But in the meantime he was going to make sure one and all knew that Mustafat was a wanted cat, and as a result of his actions, special arrangements were now being made to capture Lucif.

Once down stairs, Fred and Charlie prepared to leave. Filo had opened the large doors that led straight out onto the street and they took to the skies, heading for the barge where Stanton lived. Having secured the doors, Filo walked over to the broom cupboard and opened the trap door.

"Anklesnap, I know you can hear me. You and that cat Mustafat are in big trouble now, and I know that bumbling cat Mustafat is working for Lucif. So all the animals in all the land are now looking for Lucif. Saber, Foil, I know you can hear me. You have now one thing to look forward to and that is your punishment when you are caught. Believe me, it is so bad I shudder every time I think about it. Belvedere, don't worry. The very best is coming to save you. You hear that, Mustafat, the very best."

Filo's voice echoed down the sewers, and sure enough it reached Mustafat, Anklesnap and Saber and Foil. Belvedere, who was hanging upside down tied to a pole that was being carried by Saber and Foil, listened and a great smile beamed across his face. He knew what Filo meant. Fred and Charlie were coming to save him.

Mustafat had stopped to listen to Filo Mackay's voice and fear ran through his body like an out of control steam engine. Seeing this Anklesnap walked over to the now very scared cat and hissed in his face. "Don't you think anything, Mustafat. You are Lucif's little runner. You have done his dirty work and after this you will have no use. Ha, ha, ha, ha."

The ferret laughed as he continued along the sewer. Filo had been right and as Saber and Foil walked past him so as not to lose sight of Anklesnap, they turned to Mustafat.

"We warned you. You got us into this, you get us out of it. If we are alive or not spending the next hundred years in prison, we want nothing more to do with you."With that they walked on, leaving Mustafat to think, until, that is, it began to get dark because Anklesnap had the torch and then he hurried along to catch up with them. As they made their way to Lucif's secret hideout no one spoke.

Sweeney and Todd had only just made it back to the Tower. Spotting Ripper was easy, as he was the only raven left on the roof of one of the buildings at the Tower. Slowly he swept as Sweeney and Todd landed. Throwing down his brush, he raced over to them to find out what they had discovered and if they had seen Lucif.

Sweeney and Todd were out of breath and obviously very flustered as they began to explain to Ripper what had happened.

"Oh Ripper, you are in so much trouble. We met with Lucif. Horrible he is, tall and mean he is, darts on his jacket that he throws, tools of pain that would scare you to the bone, screams of pain coming from somewhere inside his hideout, and fishy breath that would turn milk to yogurt."

Ripper rolled his eyes. How could Sweeney and Todd be frightened of Lucif and where he lived considering where they lived? Uninterested, he told them to continue.

"Ripper, we have a message for you. Lucif knows that you wrote the message on the wall for the pigeons and he says he is going to come after you later."

Ripper's feathers turned a very funny shade of grey with fear. Lucif was after him. This was not in his plan. Now he really had to get his wings on the title and the book The Great London Adventure. And, as Sweeney and Todd continued, his evil mind began to work. Sweeney and Todd told Ripper that on their way to see him they had heard that Mustafat, who was working for Lucif, had captured Belvedere. A smile grew across Ripper's beak. This was the chance he had been waiting for, news that he could pass on to Hector that would build his trust in him and ensure that he was close to Fred and Charlie when they returned - if they returned!

He had to act quickly. Thanking Sweeney and Todd, who were going home to the safety of their dungeon, Ripper told them as they left not to worry, but they were not convinced. Ripper travelled as fast as he could to Hector's office. Pounding on the door, he waited for Hector to shout enter and sure enough Hector's voice rang out, 'Enter'.

Once inside, Ripper explained everything Sweeney and Todd had told him. Hector, being as wise as he was, telephoned The Great Gob, who confirmed the news. Bostrum was shocked and immediately sprang into action.

"Prepare the dining room. Get my equipment. I am going to help my sons,"he shouted. Thanking Ripper for the news, he left Hector's office with Honourous by his side. Hector also thanked Ripper and told him to go and help Bostrum. Ripper's plan had worked. He was safe with all the ravens around him and he was close to hand if Fred, Charlie and Belvedere should return.

The two brothers were making good time and Stanton's barge was not far away. They hoped that Belvedere was going to be all right and no harm would come to him. Belvedere, who was still tied to the pole that Saber and Foil were carrying, thought of Fred and Charlie. He knew they would not let him down.

10
chapter

The old war dog advises

The flight to Stanton's was difficult and was one that Fred and Charlie could have done without. The crosswinds meant that keeping a straight line was very difficult. But for Belvedere they would do anything. Charlie seemed to be very annoyed with the satchel, but Fred did not say anything as he knew his brother was missing Belvedere. They had become quite close and Charlie had enjoyed the responsibility of having him as a passenger.

Time had passed quickly and as the morning sun rose Fred and Charlie suddenly realised that another day had gone by and that the clock was ticking as they tried to ensure the safe return of the little Gronk.

Down below Stanton's barge could be seen, moored on a viaduct called the Seven Arches that carried the Grand Union Canal. As the two brothers flew past, they noticed that the deck of the barge was littered with old fridges and televisions and army flags of different regiments flew all the way down the sides. The barge was clearly named in bright gold paint 'The Hound's Barracks'. Fred and Charlie knew that they had found the right place.

The only place Fred and Charlie could find to land was on the water. If they tried to land on the embankment they were sure to become entangled in the many television aerials stuck in the ground. They had landed many times on the waters in the fountains in Trafalgar Square, so both felt confident that they could manage the canal.

As Fred and Charlie came in to land they soon realised that the canal was as not as calm as the waters in the fountains and judging when they would touch the water was very difficult, but they had to land. Fred was the first to touch the water, but as he did so his feet went under the water causing him to dive head first. Charlie, who was very close behind, became entangled in Fred's feet that were now sticking out of the water. Together they both went under. Water sprayed everywhere and the sound of beating wings against the water echoed around the canal banks. To Fred and Charlie's amazement they came to a slow stop and, raising their beaks out of the water, they began coughing and spluttering. They were down, but only just alive, another few feet and they would have drowned. As Fred and Charlie tried to stay afloat a large head of a wrinkled dog greeted them. As he looked at them over the side of the barge, he began to laugh.

"So, what do we have here? What on earth do you think you are playing at? That is no way to land. Amateurs," said the old dog as he threw Fred and Charlie a rope and pulled them aboard his barge. Standing on the barge soaked through, Fred and Charlie looked round at the hundreds of televisions, washing machines and hoovers that lay scattered across the deck. None of them obviously worked as wires came from every side of every appliance. Handing Fred and Charlie a dirty oily rag, the old dog with the wrinkled face sat down and adjusted his screwdrivers in his top pocket.

"Stanton's the name. Colonel Stanton, that is. I take it you are the two ravens that Filo told me about on the radio. Something to do with the fact that you have to save your friend Belvedere or something from Lucif. Well, that should be no problem, but you will need training, do you hear, training."

In fact Fred and Charlie were finding it very difficult to hear with all the water in their ears, but with one quick shake of their heads their hearing was back to normal. Fred and Charlie explained to Stanton exactly what had happened and how Filo thought he might be able to help.

"Yes, yes, yes I can help, but I think you need to come inside and dry off," said the old war dog, in a snappy way. Getting to his paws Stanton showed Fred and Charlie down below decks that turned out to be just as cluttered with televisions and old wiring. Stanton very quickly cleared a place for Fred and Charlie to sit, but before they could get too comfortable they had to change their clothes. Stanton had found some old army uniforms that would fit them and, whilst they changed, the old dog cooked breakfast and made some fresh tea. Placing the plates of food in front of Fred and Charlie, Stanton sat down.

"Well, eat up, it is only sausage and bread, but it will do you good," said Stanton who had nearly finished his. It had been the first time that Fred and Charlie had eaten sausages, but they found them very good and had soon licked their plates clean. Pushing the plates to one side, Stanton took out his notebook and pencil.

"So Mustafat is around, is he. Every time I hear his name I just want to bark. In fact I will." Stanton let out a very loud bark, and shook his head from side to side. "There, that's better. Now, where were we? Ah.Yes, we have to get you trained and fit for the meeting at London Zoo with Mustafat and Lucif. Dangerous operation this, and we don't have much time. Never mind, I think I can do it." Stanton hurriedly made some notes, before placing his pencil behind his ear. "Right, I am going to teach you to move without being heard. I am going to teach you the art of feather control in flight. Then I am going to teach you beak Morse code, how to communicate without speaking, and then I am going to teach you how to fly as you have never been able to fly before. Do you understand?"

"Yes," said Fred and Charlie, amazed at how much they had to learn in such a short time.

"Yes, sir," corrected Stanton, who had walked over to a most peculiar object covered with a blanket. Removing the blanket, Fred and Charlie saw to their surprise a beautifully coloured bird sat upon a perch. It started to chatter in a strange language. Taking the bird from his perch, Stanton told him to fly to the Tower of London and tell Hector that Fred and Charlie were safe and sound and that he was training them. The brightly coloured bird winked at Fred and Charlie and flew straight out of one of the tiny round windows.

"Right, now then, word has been sent to the Tower that you are in good hands, but we have to start your training straight away."

Stanton placed a Green Beret on his head and ordered his new recruits to their feet. Not wishing to argue, Fred and Charlie did as they were told.

"Left, right, left, right, left, right," ordered Stanton as the three of them marched back out onto the deck of the barge.

Deep down below, in the sewers of London, Mustafat had found a few added problems on his journey. His paws kept getting stuck in the drain covers and every now and then Saber and Foil had to stop and pull his paw free, much to their annoyance. Finally they had arrived back at Lucif's hideout.

Anklesnap explained to Lucif what Mustafat had done and what Filo had shouted down the sewers at them. The meanest cat of the whole of London was very unhappy with Mustafat and, as he scowled at him, Mustafat was certain his eyes turned red. Saber and Foil kept very quiet as they could see that the slightest thing and Lucif might turn very nasty.

"So, you fool, you come here with that Gronk and no ravens and then you get me involved in kidnapping, you fool. What use is a Gronk to me? And to choose London Zoo, a place where nice animals live peacefully! Fool!" shouted Lucif. For once in his life Mustafat said nothing, his idol had turned on him. Saber and Foil were right. They should have gone home. Hanging his head low, Mustafat waited with flat ears to hear his fate as once again Lucif raised his voice.

"There is nothing else for it. I will have to go to the Zoo later and sort this mess out, but in the meantime you had better take that Gronk with you, Mustafat. If anything happens to him, I shall deal with you personally. Anklesnap, take Petula with you. Omph, fetch her. Anklesnap, make sure these three don't lose the Gronk or the rabbit," hissed Lucif as Anklesnap led Mustafat, Saber and Foil from the room. Petula, who also had been tied to a pole, joined Belvedere, who had been left outside. Saber and Foil now had two poles to carry and set off down the sewers to London Zoo. They hissed at Mustafat, who was trying to be friends with them again. Silence fell and Mustafat felt very lonely as he followed Anklesnap, who was leading the way.

Hector, Bostrum, Honourous and Sledger had all gathered in the dining room and Ripper had been placed at the door to keep guard. The brightly coloured bird that Stanton had sent flew through an open window and landed on the large table in front of all the ravens. Ripper turned and went to stop the bird, but was stopped by Hector as it began to speak.

"Hello, my name is Cassiquaire. I have been sent to you by Stanton, the old war dog."

Hector welcomed the little bird and Bostrum asked what he

wanted. Cassiquaire passed on the message of how Fred and Charlie were now in training and that they would be fine. Stanton was going to teach them all he knew. Bostrum had heard about Stanton and knew that if he was training his sons then they would be elite crack ravens by the time he had finished. With the message safely delivered, Cassiquaire took to the air and flew off.

Bostrum and Hector watched as Cassiquaire flew out of the window and over the Tower walls. Sledger, who had returned with some food and something to drink, had caught the last part of what Cassiquaire was saying before he had flown off. Placing the tray down on the table, Sledger looked over at Bostrum, who seemed to be a little more relaxed.

"Fred and Charlie have been already trained by Bostrum, but when they finish this training, they will be the highest trained ravens at the Tower," said Hector, trying to break the silence that had fallen over the room. Ripper, who had been listening, was now very concerned. If Fred and Charlie were that highly trained, how was he going to capture them and steal the book and the title? Just then, as Bostrum left the dining room, Ripper saluted, but as Hector walked past, he told Ripper to put on his fighting uniform. They were all going to help Fred and Charlie, training or no training. Sledger and Ripper now stood alone in the dining room.

"Why are we going to war?" said Ripper, as Sledger cleaned up.

"Because it is our duty to help fellow ravens that's why,

Ripper. What's the matter? Are you scared?"

Ripper shook his head, curled his beak up and left Sledger to go and put his fighting uniform on. The truth was that Ripper was scared.

Fred and Charlie had never worked so hard in their lives. Up and down the embankment of the canal they walked, trying to keep their feathers quiet, and every time they made a noise Stanton would bark at them. What did he know, thought Charlie, he had no feathers and did not know how difficult it was to keep them quiet even under their uniforms. But he knew how important the training was and kept on trying.

"Boo," shouted Fred and Charlie leapt into the air. He wondered how Fred had crept up behind him so quietly. Fred had mastered the art of keeping his feathers silent and before long the two brothers were creeping up behind each other without making a sound. Stanton was very pleased with them and admired Charlie for trying until he too had mastered the art of silent movement.

Stanton called the two brothers in for lunch. The sandwiches that he had made soon vanished. Fred and Charlie were very hungry after all the work they had done that morning. Letting their food digest, Fred and Charlie listened to Stanton's war stories of when he was in the Special Dog Service, the elite regiment of the dogs' army. Fred and Charlie listened with great interest and wished one day that they would experience some of the things he had, but then, as he pointed out, they were about to take on the meanest cat of all time.

With lunch and Stanton's stories out of the way, it was back down to the hard training. Stanton had placed in front of Fred and Charlie a book with dots and dashes in it and explained that this was Morse Code. To his right Stanton turned on a radio and it burst into life.

"This is the BBC World service."

Stanton looked in total surprise at the radio and immediately went to work with his screwdriver. At last the radio began to make beeping noises, some long and some short. The old war dog began explaining that Fred and Charlie could mimic the noises with their beaks and by making a squeaking noise in their throats. Fred and Charlie tried, and sure enough they could make the noise.

"There you go, told you. You can now learn Morse Code. You see each letter is built up of dots and dashes. For example, dot dash or beep beeeep is the letter A. Now you try."

Fred and Charlie found making the noises no problem at all and in no time were learning the code of Morse letter by letter. Stanton then explained that if they joined letters together they formed words and with words they could speak to each other without Mustafat, Lucif or anyone else understanding what they were saying. That was, of course, if they could not speak Morse, but very few animals in London did, so Stanton was quite certain they would be safe.

The two brothers practised and practised building up words and trying to understand what each other was saying whilst Stanton sat back and read his paper the Daily Hound. Just then there was a knock from the deck above and Stanton told Fred and Charlie to continue whilst he found out who it was. A few minutes later Stanton returned carrying bags of shopping and as Stanton began to unpack the bags he introduced Fred and Charlie to his wife, 'The Duchess'.

Acknowledging Fred and Charlie, the Duchess turned on Stanton and told him that she had never seen so much mess and that it would take her the rest of the day to clean it all up. Stanton muttered under his breath about how much time and money the Duchess spent at Prescows the store round the corner as he began to help wash the plates that they had used for lunch. Pushing Stanton out the way, the Duchess told him to take Fred and Charlie outside and teach them there. Fred and Charlie got up and followed Stanton outside. He was still muttering under his breath.

Belvedere wondered why they had stopped and then suddenly realised that, they were waiting under a large drain cover that, judging by all the strange sounds of animals, was under London Zoo. Mustafat, Anklesnap, Saber and Foil were waiting for all the zookeepers to leave so that they could sneak in. Mustafat was tempted to open the drain and breathe some fresh air, but he knew it would be too much of a risk. Saber, who had released Petula's and Belvedere's bindings, asked them if they were all right and could he get anything for them. Both of them nodded and, as he removed the tape that was covering their mouths, they both asked for him to set them free. Much as he wished he could, Saber told them that it was impossible and once again covered their mouths so they did not shout out and draw attention to them all hiding in the sewer.

Mustafat and Anklesnap both fell asleep and Saber saw his chance to help Belvedere and Petula. Releasing the tape on their mouths, he told them that if they were quiet he would leave it off. Belvedere and Petula agreed and were thankful for his help.

"You know Fred and Charlie are going to save me and when they do, all the animals in London are going to be against you," whispered Belvedere, but Saber and Foil would not listen. They knew the trouble they were in and how much everyone was going to hate them, but what could they do, except wait and see what happened? Belvedere winked at Petula and told her not to worry, making her smile. Even though the Gronk knew it was a brave smile it made him feel better.

Fred and Charlie had mastered the art of Morse Code and were really quite good at it. Stanton, who was sitting down on an old television, got to his feet and tried to look busy as the Duchess came up on deck.

"Right, I have done the cleaning up and now I am off to the bingo. Now, you keep things clean down there. The place looks like a workshop instead of a home."

Stanton grunted a good-bye as the Duchess said her farewells to Fred and Charlie and, as she walked off down the tow path at the side of the canal, the two brothers could hear Stanton muttering inside the barge amongst a lot of banging and clattering.

"Comes along and tidies everything up, can't find a thing, keep it clean, she says. Huh, how can I keep it clean, when I can't find anything?"

From inside the barge all the banging and muttering had stopped and Stanton appeared on the deck of the barge carrying two hoovers. Fred and Charlie wondered what he was up to.

"Now then, for your next bit of the training. You have done very well, but this is the tricky part," said Stanton plugging the machines in.

"Found these in a rubbish bin when I was out on one of my walks. They should work," shouted Stanton as he turned them on. The noise was deafening as the hoovers came to life. Stanton picked up the hoover hose and the characteristic folds of his face were suddenly sucked into the pipe. As Stanton wrestled with the pipe, Fred and Charlie looked on in horror. They did not know what to do for the best - laugh and let the old war dog sort things out for himself, or help him. But Stanton's face was being sucked further into the pipe and was now making a very loud raspberry noise. Finally he reached the off switch and the hoovers lost their power before stopping. With a loud plop Stanton pulled his face free, looking slightly embarrassed.

"Yes, well they work now. I was meant to turn this switch so that they blew air instead of suck, you see. I will turn these on and you will fly into the blowing air. This will build you strength up."

But Fred and Charlie were laughing. Stanton's face had a large red ring on it where the hose of the hoover had sucked his face inside. Stanton not very amused at Fred and Charlie's outburst. He switched the hoover on and blew them down the towpath.

"Tun it off, turn it off," shouted the two brothers. Stanton turned the hoover off and Fred and Charlie landed in a heap.

"That will teach you to laugh at others," shouted Stanton as Fred and Charlie rose to their feet. Switching on the hoover again, the air began to blow and Fred and Charlie took to the air, only flying a few feet above the ground.

Hours passed as Fred and Charlie continued their training. Stanton had them flying in all different ways and aimed the blowing air at them from the side, underneath and straight on. It was very exhausting, but Fred and Charlie could feel the benefits and knew that whatever weather they flew in in the future, it would be easy. They were becoming top raven flyers.

Through the night they trained, resting only when they felt

they could not fly anymore, then it was down to more Morse beak training and learning plans of London. Although very tired, when Fred and Charlie finally got to bed in the very early hours of the morning they felt like new ravens and able to take on Lucif. Stanton had told them that he would wake them for the final briefing before they left for London Zoo.

Belvedere had been awoken by the sound of the drain cover being removed. The Zoo above them was still now and apart from the noises that some of the animals made, the coast was clear. Saber and Foil passed the poles carrying Belvedere and Petula up to Mustafat and Anklesnap. Once out of the sewer, everyone breathed in the night air that smelt so refreshing. Mustafat would have given anything to have a bath, even though he was not very keen on water.

Anklesnap led the way through the Zoo, and as they passed large open enclosures, animals watched as they walked by. Mustafat, Saber and Foil sensed how happy all the animals were, they were well fed and had plenty of space to play. Very different to the cellar at the Royal Albert Hall where Mustafat, Saber and Foil lived and these animals did not have a loud noisy boiler keeping them up all night, thought Mustafat.

Seeing a wall, Mustafat thought that he would have a look over and see who lived behind, against Anklesnap's advice. Once on the wall Mustafat froze. Coming towards him was a branch that was moving all on its own, almost as if it was sniffing for something. Then the branch let out an almighty noise. Mustafat puffed himself up like a ball of wool as two huge eyes appeared behind the branch. It was not a branch at all, thought Mustafat, it was the trunk of an elephant. As Mustafat jumped down Anklesnap turned on him.

"That's it. Let everyone know we are here. Stop teasing the animals. Some of them are endangered species and deserve a lot of respect, so stop acting the fool and come on."

Mustafat was shocked at Anklesnap's attitude and did not like being spoken to in such a way. Facing the ferret, Mustafat stood his ground.

"Just remember that I work with Lucif and, if I want to, I can get you into very serious trouble."

The ferret fell about laughing, much to Mustafat's disgust. "You get me into trouble? I don't think so. Lucif and I escaped together from Trickston Nick, the big prison, so I think he will take my side before yours. Lucif has asked me to keep an eye on you three and make sure our Gronk and rabbit do not escape. Once this is all over you, Ripper, and all the others that Lucif has had a problem with are in for a very long journey, never to be seen again."

Anklesnap moved on leaving Mustafat speechless. Saber and Foil followed. They had already had enough of Mustafat and the more he tried to be the big cat the more they disliked him. With Mustafat at the rear Anklesnap finally brought them to a halt.

"There it is. This is where we meet Lucif tomorrow. All we have to do is get the Gronk and the rabbit over to that island and we can rest until he arrives."

Anklesnap was pointing at an island in the middle of a large enclosure surrounded by water. The water round the island was not deep, just cold, and in no time at all everyone was settled and Anklesnap had returned with some food that he had stolen from the rubbish bins. Belvedere and Petula had been told that there was no escape and that Lucif's bodyguards were all around even though they could not see them. Belvedere and Petula were just glad to be free from the poles that had carried them there and sat next to each other.

Saber, Foil and Anklesnap, under the latter's instructions, had built a hideout so no one could see them. They had a long wait till the next night and they did not want to attract too much attention from the zookeepers and other animals and especially the Rucksacks, which Belvedere was sure to do.

By the time everyone was settled on the island it was nearly five-thirty in the morning. Fred and Charlie had been asleep for about an hour and Bostrum, Ripper, Sledger, Hector and many of the other ravens had been planning all night. The plans for the following days had been made and take-off time would be about seven o'clock that night. Hector and Bostrum had a full squadron of ravens going out to help Fred and Charlie.

Mustafat, Saber, Foil and Anklesnap, having eaten the

leftover food, drifted off to sleep and Belvedere and Petula did the same, knowing that there was no chance of escape. The night that lay ahead was going to be very important in the history of the animal kingdom of London and rest was required so all had their strength.

11
chapter

Fred and Charlie are on their way

Stanton had been up since the call of the early morning cockerel. He had decided to leave Fred and Charlie sleeping after their hard training the day before, but now the time had come for them to rise as they still had lots to do. In true army style Stanton filled a bucket of water, walked into the room where Fred and Charlie were still sleeping, and threw the bucket of water over them.

"Rise and shine, let's have you up and at them," shouted Stanton as he marched up to them and began shaking them furiously. Fred and Charlie could not believe what Stanton had just done. They were drenched from head to foot. Having no option but to get up, Fred and Charlie walked to the bathroom where they found a fresh set of dry clothes. Stanton could be heard in the kitchen making breakfast, and the two brothers wished that he could whistle properly. With a quick change of clothes and a wash of their beaks the two brothers felt amazing and ready to take on Lucif.

As they sat down at the breakfast table, Stanton placed in front of them a huge breakfast. Fred and Charlie, who were very hungry, took no time at all in clearing their plates. The old war dog sat down and joined his two recruits. The Duchess had gone shopping and this left Stanton free all day to finish Fred and Charlie's training. He explained that they would cover everything that they had learnt the day before and finish off with some very tactical training. Fred and Charlie could not wait to get outside and begin, but before they did, Stanton wanted to make sure that they still remembered their Morse Code. Fred and Charlie chatted away in Morse for nearly an hour and Stanton understood what they were saying. They did not make one mistake at all.

In London Zoo Belvedere awoke to the sound of strange animals and Mustafat, Saber and Foil talking. Anklesnap had gone to get word to Lucif and find some more food. Hidden behind the screen of branches and leaves, Belvedere could not see what was going on in the Zoo. Petula sat very quietly next to the little Gronk. She was very tired and very worried.

Mustafat was getting anxious and was playing with old leaves and twigs. "I have had more fun looking through rubbish bins than waiting around like this." Looking over at Belvedere he wondered if all this boredom and trouble was worth it.

Saber, who was now very annoyed with Mustafat, looked at him in a menacing way. "So tell me, great Mustafat, why do you think that Lucif is interested in teaming up with you? If he wanted the Gronk why did he not just go and get him? And if he wanted ravens then why did he not just go down to the Tower and grab himself one or two? No, it is like the little Gronk said last night. We have been used."

Mustafat shot to his feet and took hold of Saber by the scruff of his neck. "Don't ask me questions like that. I don't know. Great minds think alike and all that sort of stuff, I guess."

Just then Anklesnap returned in time to have his say. "Don't trust a word he says, Saber and Foil. I will tell you the answer's to your questions. Lucif has used you all and Mustafat has guided you into a war zone by thinking that Lucif is going to team up with him. Huh, Lucif does not need him. If all of this goes wrong dear Mustafat there, will take the blame and that is exactly what he is going to do, because Lucif will make sure he does, and you two are going to take the blame as well. Lucif will become Grand Master and hold the book of The Great London Adventure. As for you three getting Fred, Charlie and this Gronk, no way. He has plans for them and that includes Petula."

Mustafat's mouth fell open. The truth was out. Lucif had used him for his own means. The silly cat had been fooled and he did not know what to do! Jumping to his feet, Mustafat shook his paw at Anklesnap.

"I want to see Lucif now, do you understand me, now," he shouted at the top of his voice. Anklesnap simply laughed and told him to sit down, throwing him a roll. Mustafat did as he was told and ate the roll in silence. Foil offered Petula and Belvedere some of his food and everyone sat in silence.

"'Morning Bostrum," said Hector as he rose from one of the dining room benches. With a great big stretch he watched as Bostrum worked on a route plan with Honourous. Fray and Bentos, the Tower's chefs, had cooked a lovely breakfast some time before and Hector satisfied himself with the left over's. Sledger entered the dining room to give Hector his morning report.

"Nothing to report, Hector. All the guards have retired for some sleep and the day-duty ravens are entertaining the Rucksacks. All is ready for the crowning of Fred, Charlie and Belvedere, if they make it back."

The room fell silent, 'If Fred, Charlie and Belvedere made it back'. The very words that no one had dared mention. Sledger, realising his mistake, corrected himself, 'when they made it back'. Bostrum, wanting to change the subject, coughed and asked who was going to London Zoo that night.

Hector knew that decisions like these always fell on his shoulders and he had to be precise. After thinking for a while, he rose to his feet. He might be old, but he still could take command when he wanted to.

"Right. Ripper will lead us in. Copey will have to come because of his tactical mind. Bostrum, you will fly second in line in the formation. I have selected four other ravens that all have battle experience: Topy, Crackers, Fiddler and Scotty. You have the best there, Sledger. Honourous and I will remain here and make sure that everything is organised for your return."

Bostrum was very impressed with Hector's leadership skills, but then he was the Chief of all the ravens and this was one of the reasons. Turning round, Bostrum and Hector noticed that Bascer had entered the dining room and in his arms he carried a large pile of clothes. Placing them on the table, Bascer explained that he had made new uniforms for everyone that was going to help Fred, Charlie and Belvedere. Hector was very proud of Bascer and, as he set to work fitting the uniforms to ensure that they fitted snugly, he sent word to send a very large bunch of flowers to Bascer's wife as he was certain that she had worked all night.

Belvedere was feeling a lot better now that he had eaten some food and had a drink and he hoped that Fred and Charlie would not take long before they came to rescue him. Mustafat sat in the corner, muttering to himself. Saber and Foil, however, were thinking of how they could escape with Belvedere and Petula and return them back to the Tower in the hope that The Great Gob might pardon them for their involvement in Lucif's plans. But it was no use. Anklesnap kept a close eye on his prisoners.

"YEPPPPPPPEEEEEEEEEEEEEEEEEEEEE," cried Charlie as he flew down the canal practising his low-level flying, followed closely by Fred. They were flying so fast that behind them their wings caused the canal to rise in a spray. Then it was heard. A loud crack of air as once again they flew past Hector. Fred and Charlie had flown Ravenonic, the fastest a raven could fly. Stanton clapped his paws together and told Fred and Charlie to land. Landing perfectly Fred and Charlie touched down to report to Stanton.

"Stand to attention, chaps," ordered Stanton, as he walked behind Fred and Charlie with his paws clasped behind his back. "Good, good, very good. You have done very well with your training and as a result of your brilliant flying and the skills that you have learnt here, it gives me great pleasure to award you the honour of wearing the Cherry Beret, only ever given to one raven before and that was Pathfinder."

Stanton placed the berets on Fred and Charlie, making sure that they fitted and were at the right angle. Stanton then issued Fred and Charlie with their new uniforms. They looked so highly trained in their green combat green jackets and with their very fine Cherry Berets fitted on their heads.

Fred and Charlie saluted Stanton and requested permission for a fly past to celebrate. Stanton gave them permission and Fred and Charlie took to the air.

Woooshhh, through the air they flew and with the skills of true flyers Fred and Charlie did a victory roll. Banking round, the two brothers came into land to the applause of Stanton. Final preparations now had to be made and the old war dog issued Fred and Charlie with their final kit. Water bottles with long straws were hung round the necks of Fred and Charlie so they could drink whilst in flight. Head torches were packed in pockets so they could fly safely at night, flares were strapped to their shoulders just in case they needed them in an emergency. Packed and looking very strong Fred and Charlie were ready.

Little did Mustafat, Anklesnap, Saber and Foil know about how much training Fred and Charlie had gone through. If they did, perhaps they would have considered letting the little Gronk go. Just then, came a rustle from behind the bushes and Mustafat stood up. Anklesnap looked over at him and smiled. Lucif had arrived.

"Told you everything was alright. Belvedere and Petula have been very quiet, and Mustafat, well, he has been moaning," said Anklesnap as Lucif stepped into sight from the cover of the bushes. Lucif smiled and praised his old friend on the good job that he had done. Looking over at Mustafat Lucif's eyes grew red as they had done before.

"Well, Mustafat, so you thought that I was going to be your partner. FOOL. You are going to take all the blame for the capture of Belvedere and Petula, whilst I become Grand Master and I will own the book The Great London Adventure that is full of secrets and places where riches are held."

Laughing in an evil tone, Lucif sat down next to Anklesnap. Mustafat's temper rose and, as he got to his feet, he pulled a piece of rope from his pocket. Lucif could not get away with this, he thought. As he stepped forward to lunge at the master criminal, two of Lucif's bodyguards tackled him to the ground and sat on him. Saber and Foil were shocked at Mustafat's bravery.

Mustafat, who now was very uncomfortable with the weight of the two bodyguards on him, squealed to be released, but Lucif ordered him to be tied up. Saber and Foil dared not speak as Mustafat pleaded not to be tied up. Lucif agreed that if he sat quietly and did not say another word he would not tie him up. Mustafat did as he was told and sat very still.

A clock chimed in the background. It was seven o'clock in the evening. The Zoo was closed and now Lucif could get on with the business he had to take care of and that was dealing with Fred and Charlie.

As Ripper led the way, Bostrum and all the other ravens that Hector had ordered were flying across London to London Zoo. They looked so very impressive flying in formation.

Fred and Charlie were ready for take off, their destination London Zoo, a place that represented freedom for animals, a place where great care and attention were taken for the protection of animals, a place were Belvedere would be reunited with his friends.

The two brothers felt very confident and, with a final salute to Stanton, Fred and Charlie were airborne. Stanton, with his army pack on his back, started the barge's engines and began to make his way down the canal to the Serpentine and on to the Zoo. The Duchess was downstairs making sandwiches for her brave Stanton and his now fully trained ravens for when they had finished with Lucif and his gang. Fred and Charlie, who were flying high above, looked down and Stanton who gave them a final wave.

All the Zoo keepers were finishing their rounds, making sure that all the animals had enough food and water for the night, and as the last bale of hay was left out for reserves for some of the animals, a loud clunk of the gates' bolts echoed across the Zoo.

Lucif rubbed his hands together as he unpacked the hamper of food that Omph had made for him earlier. Starting with his homemade fish cakes, Lucif began to eat whilst all around him watched, their mouths watering at the delicate smells of the fine food.

The evening traffic was busy in the London streets below as Fred and Charlie began their descent towards London Zoo. Fred had suggested that they flew very low so as not to be spotted by any of Lucif's lookouts and Charlie was now beginning to understand why they had been through all the training. He felt so wonderful and proud to be a Yeoman raven.

Bostrum had already arrived at the Zoo and had landed on the main gates' roof. Ripper, who had enjoyed the flight, was now feeling very nervous as they all took up their positions to wait for Fred and Charlie. Suddenly a pigeon landed next to Bostrum and handed him a note wishing him well from Plodger. All the animals in London were behind Fred and Charlie and hoped that they defeated Lucif. Suddenly Ripper nudged Bostrum. He had spotted Fred and Charlie. As the two brothers flew very low over their father, he puffed his chest out. He was so proud of his sons.

"Alpha One to Alpha Two, this is a radio check," crackled Fred's radio.

"Er, Roger that, Alpha One, radio check complete. Landing required, runway clear and flaps are down. Did you see our Father?"

"Yes, Fred, I did, and did you see the way he puffed his chest out? I think that he was very proud," replied Charlie as they hovered above their landing spot. Fred agreed, but told his brother that they had more important business than to find out why their father was there and to talk to him. Charlie acknowledged Fred's comment as they landed with the elegance of two Harrier jets. Safely on the ground, Fred and Charlie ran for cover.

Omph burst through the bushes nearly making Lucif choke with surprise. "They are here, Lucif. Fred and Charlie are here," shouted Omph.

Lucif rose to his feet throwing his sandwiches to one side. "Where are they" questioned Lucif with an evil glint in his eye. Omph told him that they were by the main gates and that some other ravens had arrived as well. Lucif sprang into action, ordering Omph to keep guard of Belvedere, Petula, Mustafat, Saber and Foil. Lucif stood with his paws pointing to the sky. "My finest hour is about to happen. Soon I will be Grand Master of all the animals and hold all the secrets of London."

Omph gathered Belvedere, Mustafat, Petula, Saber and Foil together and moved them into the middle of the island so that they could be seen from the main promenade of the Zoo. Then, all of a sudden, all the animals in the Zoo became restless. The hyenas chuckled, the monkeys wailed, and the elephants blew their trunks. Lucif ordered Mustafat to go and sit on a wall and whistle if he saw the ravens. More out of fear than wanting to help Lucif, Mustafat did as he was told.

Fred and Charlie now realised that Lucif must know that they had arrived with all the commotion the animals were causing. Bostrum stood up on the end of his claws, trying to see what was going on. He could not see Lucif, but at least he could still see his sons. Suddenly Fred's radio crackled.

"Fred Alpha One, this is Stanton Alpha Base Three. I have arrived in position and am here if you should need me."

"Roger that Base Three. We shall call you, if we need you," said Fred. The radios fell silent and Fred looked at Charlie. The time had come for them to make their way through the Zoo and confront Lucif, but just as they were about to step forward a large crow landed beside them.

"'Evening. Ghost Step is my name. Just thought that I would say if you need any help I am here for you. Good luck."

Not giving Fred and Charlie the chance to answer, Ghost

Step flew off, leaving the two brothers pleased, but also concerned. Walking forward, Fred and Charlie noticed that in a large enclosure sat a gorilla. Fred and Charlie walked over to him.

"So what brings you two here," asked the gorilla placing a large hand on his chin as he sat down.

"We have come to save our friend Belvedere the Gronkiedoddle," said Fred, being as polite as he could. The large gorilla scratched his head and thought for a while. Then, getting to his feet, walked over to an orange box at the corner of the enclosure, lifted it up and walked down some steps. Fred and Charlie watched with interest. As if by magic the large gorilla appeared from a post box opposite. Charlie took a deep breath as the large gorilla approached them. Sitting down in front of them the gorilla whispered, so no one could hear them.

"Heard a lot about you. All the animals here are talking. My name is Guy, named after my father who died in 1978. A great loss to us all he was, but anyway pleased to meet you."

Guy held out his huge hand and shook Fred and Charlie's wings. Scratching himself, Guy looked around and then leant closer to the two brothers.

"You know that Lucif is here? Everyone has been talking about it. You should stay clear of him, you know. I would love to help you find your friend, but I have bananas that I have to finish and I have to read the mice I share my bed with a bedtime story. But good luck, if you decide to go on and find your friend."

Fred and Charlie noticed Guy's reluctance to hang around, even though he was powerful enough to defeat Lucif. As the large gorilla waved goodbye, he vanished inside the post box.

Moving on, Fred and Charlie walked past the chimpanzees that were playing as usual. Fred and Charlie were amazed at how open everything was and how happy all the animals seemed. Even the rhinos seemed happy walking about and sniffing the ground. Then, just as Fred and Charlie were about to cross a large, well-kept lawn they saw Belvedere and Petula in the middle of an island in the pelican pond. Small torches burned around them and Lucif stood nearby with his arms folded across his chest. Mustafat, who was sitting on the wall in front of the pond, had not noticed Fred and Charlie yet, so they decided to take cover and survey the situation.

Once safely under a bush, Fred and Charlie watched. They could see that behind Belvedere and Petula, Saber and Foil were sitting on the grass. Lucif had not moved, but simply stood watching Mustafat. There was also no sign of Omph or any of the other bodyguards Lucif was certain to have keeping guard. All Fred and Charlie needed to do was distract Lucif, Mustafat, Saber and Foil so they could rescue Belvedere and Petula. But how were they going to do that? Just then Fred's radio crackled.

"Don't move, this is Stanton Alpha three. I am right behind you. Let me deal with Mustafat. I have an argument I want to settle with him."

"Roger that," replied Fred, being as quiet as he could. The old war dog crept his way round until he was nearly underneath Mustafat, who sat on the wall, not knowing or seeing a thing. With the skill of a true professional, Stanton swiped Mustafat with his large paw knocking him backwards. Mustafat fell into the pond only to find a huge paw lifting him out and pulling him closer to the large face of Stanton. Soaking wet, Mustafat trembled as Stanton snarled at him, "Don't make a move, Mustafat, your time is up."

Before Lucif noticed that anything was wrong Fred and Charlie took to the air. Lucif suddenly noticed the commotion and ordered his bodyguards to attack. But nobody moved. Once again Lucif shouted and still no one moved. They had all seen Stanton and they were no match for a dog like him. They had also seen how quickly Fred and Charlie were moving and knew that they could not out manoeuvre them any way.

Not giving it a second thought, Fred swooped down and struck Lucif clean in his chest with his feet. Lucif flew through the air before landing very heavily. Charlie banked round and took hold of Lucif by the scruff of his neck and Fred took hold of one of his legs. With all their might they began to lift Lucif up into the sky. Lucif tried to struggle but it was no use. Fred and Charlie had a firm grip.

Over the main gates they flew. Ripper leapt to his feet and cheered as Fred and Charlie carried Lucif further and further away. Bostrum wiped a tear from his beak. He was so proud of Fred and Charlie. They had defeated Lucif.

"On the count of three, Fred. One, two, three," shouted Charlie, and on the final count Fred and Charlie let go of Lucif. Through the air he tumbled until finally, with a big splash, he landed in the Serpentine next to Stanton's barge. Coughing and spluttering, Lucif rose to the surface and climbed onto the bank. With no bodyguards and the embarrassment of being seen to be defeated by two ravens, Lucif took to his paws. Faster and faster he ran, hopefully never to be seen again.

Fred and Charlie quickly returned to the pelican pond where they noticed that Saber and Foil were now helping Belvedere and Petula to safety. Stanton was having a wonderful time chasing what was left of Lucif's gang of bodyguards. Bostrum, Ripper and all the other ravens had flown over and were dusting down Belvedere and Petula. As soon as Fred and Charlie had landed, Ripper ran over and gave them a huge hug. They had saved his life from Lucif's evil grip and he was very grateful. Maybe this would change Ripper and he would become a better person, thought Bostrum, as he walked over to his sons.

"I am very proud of you, Fred and Charlie, and I am proud that you are my sons," said Bostrum with a tear in his eye. Fred and Charlie gave their father a hug and told him that they were proud of him too. But Fred and Charlie now turned their concern to Belvedere who stood on the ground in front of them.

"Took your time, thought you would never get here," said the little Gronk, laughing. Charlie blew his nose on the sleeve of his uniform. The emotion of seeing Belvedere was all too much for him. Petula stepped forward and kissed Charlie on the cheek, making him blush. United once again the three adventurers laughed. Now they knew that they had earned the right to be crowned Grand Masters of all the animals in London and it was time to head back to the Tower of London.

12
chapter

The crowning and wedding

No one could ever describe how Fred and Charlie felt about sending Lucif into exile. It was a moment in history and now another was about to be made, their being crowned Grand Masters.

All the animals at the Zoo were celebrating and word had quickly spread across London about Fred and Charlie's victory. Apigeon landed at the Tower and, when Hector heard the news, he leapt into the air. Taking Sledger in his arms he gave him a very big hug, much to his surprise. Fred, Charlie and Belvedere were coming home and the celebrations would soon begin. Hector ran from his office shouting at the top of his voice, "Fred and Charlie have got Belvedere. They are on their way, they are on their way."

Ravens all over the Tower squawked with delight. It had been a long time since there had been a celebration at the Tower and all the work they had all put in preparing for Fred, Charlie's and Belvedere's return and Sledger's wedding meant that this celebration would be the best the Tower had ever seen.

When Janous heard the news that their wedding was on, panic filled her. Would her wedding dress fit? Would she be ready in time? 'Oh my', she thought, in a few hours she would be Mrs Sledger. Suddenly she saw Sledger and took to her heels. He could not see her before the wedding. It was bad luck. As the door to the hospital slammed shut behind her, Sledger looked on confused. Hector placed a wing round Sledger's shoulders and offered him a reassuring hug.

Meanwhile back at the Zoo, Fred, Charlie and all the other ravens had taken to the air and formed the perfect victory formation to fly back to the Tower. The Duchess had brought Charlie's satchel from the barge before they left and Belvedere had once again taken up his rightful place as passenger in the satchel. Stanton, who had stopped chasing Lucif's bodyguards, now stood and watched as the formation of ravens with Fred and Charlie at the front flew low level over their heads. Stanton placed a paw round the Duchess's waist. He had done a good job in training Fred and Charlie and the Duchess was very proud of him, as she always was.

Saber and Foil walked through the Zoo, tired after all the running they had done escaping from Stanton's paws. As they walked into Barclays Square at the Zoo, they noticed Mustafat was sitting with his head in his paws. He looked very sad. Saber and Foil did not feel sorry for him at all, but wondered if he was going to apologise. As they walked over, Mustafat lifted his head.

"All I wanted was some respect, not this trouble," said Mustafat. But Saber and Foil still could not feel sorry for him.

"Well, Mustafat, respect is something you have to earn and not demand. So we now resign as your helpers and we want nothing more to do with you," said Saber. He nudged Foil and the two of them turned and began to walk away. Mustafat got to his feet and shouted after them. "Please wait. I know that I have been a fool and I am sorry. Can we not be friends? It would mean so much to me."

Looking back, Saber and Foil could not just forget the years that they had spent with Mustafat. Saber walked up to Mustafat and placed a paw on his shoulder.

"Okay. Look, if you promise that there are no more plans for being a Master Criminal and wanting to team up with Lucif - not that he is going to be around - we could be friends."

Mustafat agreed without hesitation and the three of them set off to the Tower in the hope that they would be allowed to watch the celebrations. Flying across London, the formation of ravens received loud applause from all the animals down below. With a victory roll here and there Fred and Charlie enjoyed themselves. Belvedere, who was looking out of his satchel, waved at everyone below. Petula had joined Stanton and the Duchess on their barge, and they were on route to the Tower of London to deliver the sandwiches that the Duchess had made earlier for Sledger's wedding, seeing that no one had eaten them after the great defeat of Lucif. It was there that Petula was going to be reunited with Filo Mackay.

Down Oxford Street Fred and Charlie flew, on to Piccadilly

Circus waving at Roadie, who was hanging out of one the windows, and on to Trafalgar Square, with a beautiful victory roll over Nelson's Column. Fred and Charlie now found themselves at the River Thames. The time had now come for Fred and Charlie to show off their low-level water flying. Telling Belvedere, Fred and Charlie began to fly as fast as they could. Belvedere, who had no fear of flying with Charlie any more, let out a cheer and the wind blew his cap off as he hung out the side of the satchel.

Ripper had never had so much fun as when the formation tried to keep up with Fred and Charlie. Water sprayed everywhere as the two brothers went Ravenonic and in no time at all the great walls of the Tower of London came into sight. Slowing down, Fred and Charlie gave the others a chance to catch up. Looking at the Tower Fred and Charlie felt a real sense of being home. Bostrum, their father, flew up beside them and told that he would now take the lead. Fred and Charlie agreed and as they flew over the walls all the ravens and many other animals that had gathered, cheered.

Hector was standing with his finest robes on, on the stage that had been built and, as the formation of ravens touched down, every one cheered even louder. A red carpet suddenly rolled out from the bottom of the stage and Fred, Charlie and Belvedere, who had climbed from the satchel, walked up towards Hector. Silence fell amongst the gathered animals and, as the three adventurers took a bow, Hector raised his wings.

"Great news, that you are home. Great news, that you have defeated Lucif. Now join me on the stage for your crowning. The Great Gob is on his way."

Fred and Charlie walked up the steps to the stage, helping Belvedere at the same time. Another huge cheer rang out as Fred, Charlie and Belvedere turned towards the crowd that was getting still larger as more and more animals were arriving at the Tower. Then Hector once again raised his wings and addressed the crowd, "Enter all Gronkiedoddles."

To the sound of tiny trumpets, thousands of Gronkiedoddles entered the Tower and lined up in front of the stage. Belvedere waved at some of his friends and Fred and Charlie recognised some of the Gronks that they had already met. Then, as a huge red curtain fell at the back of the stage, Sign-Note and his orchestra began to play. Fred, Charlie and Belvedere were so happy that they were there.

As the music came to an end, Fred and Charlie noticed that a wind had began to build and they knew that The Great Gob was on his way. Without warning, sparks burst all over the gathered crowd as Sign-Note played his last note. The Great Gob had arrived. A huge cheer rang out and everyone clapped as The Great Gob walked up and down the stage in front of Fred, Charlie and Belvedere. Ripper could not believe his eyes. He felt so proud to be part of this wonderful spectacle. Then, to his horror, he saw Sweeney and Todd in the crowd. Surely they would not carry out his plan and try and capture Fred, Charlie or Belvedere. Ripper had to do something and quickly made his way through the crowd as The Great Gob began to speak.

"Tonight we are gathered here to mark a very special occasion in the history of all the animals in London. Fred, Charlie and Belvedere have earned the right after much danger to become Grand Masters and hold the book The Great London Adventure."

The Great Gob then clapped his hands together and, as sparks flew about, the book appeared in his hands. Turning to Fred, Charlie and Belvedere, he placed the book before them. As all three held the book The Great Gob once again turned to the crowd.

"Against all the evil and bad cats of this land, Fred, Charlie and Belvedere are now to be crowned Grand Masters."

Turning once again the Great Gob placed medals on gold ribbons round Fred, Charlie and Belvedere's necks. As he did so a huge cheer rang out, and all the Gronks threw their hats into the air. Fred, Charlie and Belvedere took a step forward and took a bow. It was the best day of their lives and Bostrum looked on at his sons with a huge smile of pride. The Great Gob raised his arms and the cheering stopped.

"I now by the order given to me as ruler of all the animals in London and all the Gronkiedoddles pronounce that Fred, Charlie and Belvedere are Grand Masters."

Sign-Note and his orchestra burst into life and the music of the animal anthem played. Everyone got to their feet and sang as loudly as they could. The whole of Tower seemed to be alive with voices and music. As the anthem came to an end, The Great Gob looked over to Hector and the wise old raven took his place at the front of the stage. Clearing his throat that had become quite dry as he had never had to speak in front of so many animals before, Hector announced that the time had come for Sledger and Janous to be joined in wedlock.

Silence fell around the Tower and a very nervous Sledger began the long walk through all the animals to the front of the stage. He was dressed in his very best uniform and looked very regal. Once at the front of the stage, Fred, Charlie and Belvedere watched as he climbed the steps to stand in front of Hector. Sledger could be seen to be shaking and Fred and Charlie stood by his side for support. As Hector began to speak and utter the words of assurance to Sledger, Ripper had finally made it to where Sweeney and Todd were standing. But before he had a chance to speak, darkness enveloped him.

Duster, Buster, Tickle and Polish had sprung upon Ripper, Sweeney and Todd and covered them in sacks and pulled them up to their rooftop home. Ripper struggled with all his might, but it was no use. The four kestrels had a firm grip on the three of them. Below Duster, Buster, Tickle and Polish heard Sign-Note's orchestra beginning to play the wedding march. Although annoyed that they were going to miss the marriage of Sledger and Janous, they felt happy that they had saved Ripper from causing a disturbance with his two friends Sweeney and Todd.

As Janous made her way down the aisle created through the centre of all the animals, Sledger became very nervous. Then he noticed that Janous was standing next to him and, as he turned to look at her, he was amazed at how beautiful she looked.

Hector carried out the wedding ceremony with ease and his words could be heard all over the Tower. Animals cried with joy and many could not believe how lucky they were to see such a wonderful sight. Doc Curtious with Roadie had only just made it in time to hear Hector utter the words..

"You may kiss the bride."

Sledger and Janous kissed and once again the orchestra burst into playing their favourite piece of music. Sledger and Janous were now married.

From a safe distance Mustafat, Saber and Foil overlooked the party that followed. They had missed the crowning of Fred, Charlie and Belvedere and the wedding, because en route to the Tower they had bumped into Sam Sing, who had made them clean an alley.

The dancing and merriment went on for hours. Everyone congratulated Fred, Charlie and Belvedere and Sledger and Janous had been wished the very best by all. The Great Gob had stayed for a short while, but had left to carry on being ruler of all the animals. His duties kept him very busy.

The bells in the clock tower struck three o'clock in the morning and Sledger and Janous were preparing to leave. The music had stopped and everyone waited to see who caught Janous's bouquet. To everyone's great amusement Hector caught the bouquet and, if tradition was correct, he would be the next to marry.

But the laughter was not to last. Silence had begun to fall as a strange messenger was walking through the crowd towards Fred, Charlie and Belvedere. The tired looking Bantam handed Fred a note. The Bantam was from Wing Commander Bantam Cocksure's fleet of delivery couriers. Fred opened the note and read it aloud.

To the new Grand Masters
My Brother has told me all about
you, but now I need your help. You
must come to Paris at once and come
alone, but you must come at once

Maurice Curtious

Fred, Charlie and Belvedere looked around to see if Doc Curtious was there, but someone shouted out that he left in a hurry sometime before. A murmur began to build in the crowd as a meeting was called in Hector's office straight away. Word had been sent to The Great Gob, but first Sledger and Janous had to leave for their honeymoon.

"On with the music," shouted Hector. Sledger and Janous quickly said their goodbyes and thank you to everyone they could and to a final cheer Janous and Sledger took to the air and disappeared.

After the new Grand Masters, Bostrum and Hector had seen Sledger and Janous safely off they made their way to Hector's office. But on the way Fred and Charlie noticed that a mysterious cat was hiding on one of the roofs, and as they looked up evil menacing eyes peered back at them followed by an evil smile.

Was it Lucif?

Was it Mustafat?

Had either one of them sent the note?

Should they go to Paris?

Only Time would tell.

The End For Now......

NOTES

NOTES

NOTES

NOTES